MY SISTER THE VAMPIRE

RE-VAMPED!

Sienna Mercer

HarperTrophy®
An Imprint of HarperCollins*Publishers*

With special thanks to Josh Greenhut

My Sister the Vampire, Book Three: Re-Vamped!

Copyright © 2007 by Working Partners Limited
Series created by Working Partners Limited

www.harpercollinschildrens.com
Library of Congress Cataloging-in-Publication Data
Mercer, Sienna.
    Re-vamped! / Sienna Mercer. — 1st Harper Trophy ed.
    p.   cm. — (My sister the vampire ; #3)
    Summary: When Olivia and Ivy tell their classmates and
parents that they are identical twins, the word spreads to
the vampire officials and Olivia must prove that she is wor-
thy of keeping Ivy's true identity.
    ISBN 978-0-06-087118-5 (pbk.)
    [1. Vampires—Fiction. 2. Twins—Fiction. 3. Sisters—
Fiction. 4. Prejudices—Fiction. 5. Schools—Fiction.]
I. Title.
PZ7.M53328Re 2007   2007020826
[Fic]—dc22   CIP
                                          AC

Typography by Joel Tippie

First Harper Trophy edition, 2007

19 BRR 13

For my sister, Lisa

CHAPTER 1

"Are you done yet?" Olivia Abbott asked her mother. Olivia had finally convinced her father to take a break from his regular Tuesday tai chi-athon by shaking a pom-pom in his face, but her mom wouldn't stop embroidering the living room curtains.

"Not quite yet," her mom murmured.

"What's taking so long?" Olivia prodded.

"It's a daisy," her mom muttered, squinting with concentration, "with twenty petals."

Olivia looked at her pink glitter watch to find that less than two minutes had passed since she'd last checked. She felt like she was in a time warp—time had never moved so slowly in her entire life, and yet tomorrow was approaching at a terrifying rate. In fourteen hours and seven minutes, the *Franklin Grove Scribe,* her school paper, was going to reveal something Olivia had been keeping secret for weeks: on her first day at Franklin Grove Middle School, she had discovered a twin sister she'd never known she had. It wasn't exactly the sort of thing Olivia wanted her adoptive mom and dad to find out from the school paper.

She could not put off telling them for another minute, no matter how badly they were going to freak out.

"Mom," she said slowly, "I have to talk to you."

"Only three more petals," her mom said.

Exasperated, Olivia put her hands on her mother's shoulders and gave a gentle shake. "Attention, Mom!" she announced, like she was calling out a cheer. "This Is Your Daughter, Olivia, Speaking. I Need To Tell You And Dad Something Really, Really Important RIGHT NOW!"

"Oh, sweetheart!" her mother gasped, jumping

to her feet in concern. "I'm so sorry! You have something you need to talk about?"

Olivia's eyes rolled toward the ceiling. Parents could be so slow sometimes.

"Don't worry." Her mom took her hand. "You can tell us anything."

"Maybe you two should sit down," Olivia suggested.

Her parents exchanged nervous glances and perched on the edge of the couch. Olivia took a deep breath, and her stomach filled with butterflies. The words came spilling out as she exhaled. "On my first day at school I met Ivy and found out that she's my sister."

Olivia's mom nodded like she understood, and Olivia felt a rush of relief. Olivia had mentioned Ivy lots of times before, even though she'd never actually allowed her parents to meet her, fearing that they'd spot the resemblance right away.

"Yes, darling, and I'm very glad you're making such good friends at your new school." Her mom smiled supportively.

"Me, too." Her father gulped, looking lost.

They don't get it, Olivia thought. *This is going to*

be even harder than I expected.

"I don't mean Ivy and I are *like* sisters," she clarified. "We *are* sisters. She was born on the same day as me in Owl Creek. We were both given up for adoption when we were a year old. We're identical twins."

Olivia could almost see a flashing DOES NOT COMPUTE message suspended over her parents' heads. She decided to try another tack. Squeezing in between her mom and dad on the couch, she held out her left hand so that they could see the dark emerald ring on her middle finger.

"You know how this ring is something I got from my biological parents?" Olivia asked, looking from her mom to her dad. They both nodded. "Well, Ivy Vega has one exactly like it."

There was a long silence, and then her father began, "But how can this girl Ivy have—"

"Oh my goodness!" Mrs. Abbott interrupted. "You have an identical twin sister!" she exclaimed like she'd figured it out all on her own.

"Thank you." Olivia sighed, collapsing back into the couch. If it was this hard just to get her parents to understand that she had a *twin*, she couldn't imagine how hard it would be to explain her other huge secret: Ivy was a bona fide vampire. Luckily, Olivia wasn't going to have to explain that one, because she wasn't allowed to tell another soul that particular secret for as long as she lived.

"'I see,' said the blind man," her father intoned, sagely stroking his chin. He was always saying stuff like that, trying to sound like a kung fu master instead of an accountant.

"The adoption agency never told us you had a *sister*," her mom said. She said the word "sister" like she was saying "million dollars."

"Ivy was left at a different adoption agency," Olivia explained.

"But why would your biological parents separate you?" her mom asked. "Does Ivy know who your parents are?"

Olivia smiled. Her mom was asking all the questions she and Ivy had been trying to answer without success for weeks.

"She doesn't know," Olivia answered, "and neither does her dad," she added. "He's her only parent."

"Wow," her mom said after a moment. "I mean, wow-wee!" Olivia giggled. "How'd you two find each other after all these years?"

"I bumped into her in the hallway when I was looking for the principal's office," Olivia replied. She realized that her dad was just sitting there. "Say something, Dad. Aren't you surprised?"

He shook his head. "I always knew my little girl had a double aura." Olivia had no idea what that meant, but he seemed oddly proud. Suddenly he threw his arms around her and gave her a huge hug.

Olivia's mom clapped her hands excitedly and leaped into the hugging fray. "There's another person out there as wonderful as our daughter!" she declared happily.

"Everybody calm down!" Olivia laughed, trying to push her parents off.

"Well, I can't wait to meet her," her mom said. She stood up and straightened her blouse. "Can she come over tonight for dinner?"

Olivia glanced at her watch skeptically. "Dinner's in, like, an hour."

Her mother nodded. "Invite her father, too. I

have to meet the man who raised my daughter's sister! Do you think they like zucchini?"

Olivia shrugged. "Ivy's allergic to garlic, but I don't know about zucchini."

"Well, find out! Go call her! Shoo!" Her mom waved Olivia up the stairs as she made for the kitchen. "Come on, Steve. You can chop the vegetables with your samurai knife."

★ 🦇 ★

Ivy finally located the ringing phone buried in a pile of clothes beside her coffin. She reached in and snatched it up on the tenth ring.

"Hello?" she said, slightly out of breath.

"I told them!" her sister's voice declared.

Ivy shoved some books aside and sat down. "How'd they take it?" She and Olivia had only revealed their twinship to Toby Decker, a reporter for the school paper, on Friday, but when he'd told them that he'd succeeded in writing up the story in time to squeeze it into the upcoming Wednesday issue, the girls knew they finally had to tell their parents. At school today, Olivia had seemed almost as nervous about telling her parents as Ivy was about telling her dad.

"They are so excited about you, Ivy," said Olivia. "It was even better than when I told them I got four A's last year! What'd your dad say?"

Ivy hesitated. "Nothing."

"'Nothing' like he couldn't deal, 'nothing' like he always knew," Olivia queried, "or 'nothing' like literally nothing?"

"'Nothing' like I haven't told him yet," Ivy admitted.

"I-vyyy!" Olivia pleaded.

"Hey," Ivy said, "you left it to the last possible minute, too, remember? I was about to go upstairs and tell him when you called." Which was true. She'd been about to go upstairs for the last three hours.

"Okay, okay," Olivia said. "Do you like zucchini?"

"I guess," Ivy answered. "Why?"

"Because my mom wants you and your dad to come to our house for dinner tonight."

"I don't know if that's such a killer idea," Ivy said doubtfully. "My father barely ever eats human food . . . and I worry that meeting your parents so soon might spook him."

8

"I'll make my dad promise not to be weird," Olivia offered.

It's my *dad I'm worried about,* Ivy thought. "Would it be okay if I came by myself?" she asked. "I could use an excuse to get out of the house after I break the news."

"Sure." Olivia paused. "You're not sounding very optimistic," she pointed out, "even for a Goth."

Ivy grabbed a pillow and lay her head on it. "My adoption is my dad's least favorite topic, Olivia," she said. "Every time I bring it up, he changes the subject. And he's really old-fashioned when it comes to mixing with humans."

"You think he won't like me?" Olivia asked.

"No, he will. I know he will," Ivy replied, uncertain whether she was trying to convince Olivia or herself. "My dad has a really good heart. He'll make an exception for my blood sister. It just might take him a little while to get used to you."

"Well, he'd better," Olivia declared, "because we're stuck together."

"Like bubble gum and black licorice." Ivy

grinned. No matter what her dad was going to say, she felt lucky to have found Olivia. She took a deep breath and sat up. "Okay, I'm going to go tell him right now."

A few moments later, Ivy stood peeking in through the open door of her father's study. In the center of the bookshelf-lined room, her dad was hunched over a sprawling gray cardboard model atop a high table. From the door, Ivy could see postage stamp–sized color Xeroxes of paintings on the interior walls and elaborate floor lamps the size of chess pieces. She knew her dad was redecorating a wealthy New York family's crypt—*Vamp* magazine was already talking about doing a piece on it.

Ivy watched silently as her father adjusted a tiny gray altar in one of the rooms. Next to it, he lay a scrap of dark purple fabric as a carpet, then thought better of it and tried a burgundy one instead.

Ivy loved watching her father work. It was like watching him play with an ever-changing Goth dollhouse. She could just imagine a black-clad, high-society vampire lounging on that altar.

"Hello, Ivy," her father said suddenly without looking up.

"Hi," Ivy said in a small voice. She'd thought he hadn't known she was there.

"Is something on your mind?" he asked, picking up a tiny black coffin between thumb and forefinger.

"No." Ivy gulped. "I just thought I'd say hello. You know how I like to watch you work. That burgundy carpet's killer."

Her father glanced up at her suspiciously.

"Okay, I'd better get back to my homework and stuff," Ivy said, her heart racing. "Just wanted you to know I have an identical twin sister named Olivia who's in my science class. Bye." She bolted away.

"Ivy?" her father called after her.

She stopped in her tracks and took three slow steps backward so she could see her father again through the doorway. He was standing upright, the miniature coffin held up like a little exclamation point next to the O of his open mouth.

"What did you just say?" he asked.

"I have a twin," Ivy whispered.

"That can't be." Her father shook his head.

"Sure it can," Ivy said, trying to smile. "Her name's Olivia. She moved here at the beginning of the school year."

"And how," her father asked, "do you know this girl is your twin?"

"Because we look exactly alike," Ivy answered.

"Many people look alike," her father countered.

Ivy peered down at the emerald ring hanging from a chain around her neck. "But not many people who look like me also have a ring like mine," she pointed out.

Her father breathed in sharply through his nose. "This is . . . quite a surprise," he said slowly.

Ivy winced. "There's more," she said.

He turned a shade paler, which is no easy feat for a vampire.

Ivy steeled herself. "She's a human."

Her father gasped, and the miniature coffin slipped from his hand. He grabbed at it frantically, but it bounced off his fingers. Reaching for it, the back of his hand accidentally struck the model, and one wing's cardboard walls collapsed, crushing a pair of gargoyle easy chairs.

He stared down at the model in disbelief.

"Sorry," squeaked Ivy.

"It is not your fault," her father said absently, going to sit behind his desk. He put his head in his hands. "Does she know of your true nature?" he asked, looking up after a moment.

Of all the questions Ivy expected from her dad, this was the one she'd been dreading most. She nodded, and her father closed his eyes in disappointment.

I am going to be grounded for eternity, thought Ivy. "She would have found out sooner or later," Ivy blurted. "And Olivia won't tell anyone. She knows how serious it—"

Her father held up his hand to stop the stream of words coming from her mouth. "I understand," he said simply. He looked at her sternly, but Ivy didn't think he looked angry. He took a deep breath. "How do you feel about this sister you have found?"

"I love her," Ivy said matter-of-factly. "I couldn't imagine my life without her. I feel like meeting her was meant to be." Ivy stood there, waiting for her dad to respond, but he just stared into space. Finally she said, "Is it okay if I go to Olivia's house for dinner tonight?"

"Have you finished your homework?" her father asked expressionlessly.

"Mostly," Ivy answered.

"Then you may go," he allowed, forcing a small smile. He stood and came to give her a quick hug before looking down at his model. "It seems I have my work cut out for me here," he said, but his mind seemed to be elsewhere.

Ivy nearly skipped back down to her room in the basement. *Considering I was half expecting him to burst into flames,* she thought, *I think he took that pretty well!*

CHAPTER 2

Olivia had just finished setting the table for dinner when the doorbell rang.

"I'll get it!" her mom shouted.

Olivia immediately bolted for the front of the house and rounded the corner just in time to catch her mom swinging open the door and singing, "Hell—" her mom's voice broke mid-word "—o," she finished, mouth agape.

Olivia looked past her staring mother to see Ivy on the doorstep. Her sister had clearly dressed up for the occasion. She was wearing a warm black jacket over a turtleneck sweater, a black miniskirt with fishnets, and her long black boots.

She'd even put on her dark purple lipstick. Olivia thought she looked fabulous.

"Hi, Olivia." Ivy smiled with a worried twitch of the eyebrows toward Olivia's speechless, staring mom.

"Mom," Olivia said, elbowing her mother in the side. "This is Ivy."

"It is so . . . *interesting* to meet you, Ivy," her mom said. She glanced over Ivy's shoulder into the street. "Did your father drop you off?"

"He has to work tonight," Ivy replied. "He's really sorry he couldn't stay."

"I hope we get to meet him soon," Olivia's mom said as Olivia pushed past and gave her sister a hug.

After taking Ivy's jacket, Olivia led her into the living room, where her father did a double take. Olivia caught her mom staring at her sister's outfit again as Ivy sat down on the couch.

"Can I get you something to drab, Ivy?" Olivia's mom asked.

"You mean 'to drink,' Mom," Olivia said, completely embarrassed. Her mom was normally like America's Best Hostess, but apparently her hospitality mechanism malfunctioned when it came to guests wearing black nail polish.

Olivia stepped between Ivy and her mother and mouthed the word "sorry" to her sister. Ivy responded with a little don't-worry-about-it smile.

"Want anything?" Olivia asked aloud.

"Do you have cranberry juice?" responded Ivy.

Olivia nodded and headed for the kitchen. "I'll help you find a glass, sweetheart." Her mom gulped, hurrying after her.

Olivia groaned inwardly as she overheard her dad saying, "So, Ivy, did you know you had a double aura?"

Olivia got the bottle of cranberry juice from the fridge as her mom took down a glass.

"Is she getting over some sort of illness?" her mom whispered.

"No," Olivia said.

"I knew it!" Her mother gasped, putting her hand to her mouth. "Poor girl. Somebody died, right?"

My parents have got to get out more, Olivia thought. "No, Mom, nobody died. And Ivy's not training to be a mime, either. She's a Goth."

"Didn't Serena Star do a show about those people?" Mrs. Abbott asked.

"It's just a style choice," Olivia explained.

Her mom nodded slowly, taking this in. "Do Goths eat zucchini?" she asked.

"Yes, Mother," Olivia replied. Then she headed out of the kitchen with Ivy's drink.

A few minutes later, Mr. Abbott was staring at Olivia and her sister across the dinner table. "I wouldn't have noticed at first, but you two really do look exactly alike!" he said in amazement. "Like yin and yang."

"Like Superman and Clark Kent," Ivy agreed.

Olivia's mom set down the last casserole dish and pulled off her oven mitts. As she sat, she looked from Ivy to Olivia and smiled warmly. "Like . . . peanut butter and jelly?" she tried.

Everybody laughed. All at once, the room thawed, and Olivia's parents started showering Ivy with questions. Did she have any extracurriculars? (School newspaper.) What did her dad do for a living? (Interior designer.) What was her favorite color? (Black. Duh!)

Then Olivia's mom asked, "So, Ivy, do you have a *boyfriend*?" in that weird way mastered by moms everywhere.

Ivy squirmed in her seat as Olivia answered for her excitedly. "Yes! Brendan Daniels! He's awesome!" *Wow!* she thought as Ivy shot her a look of playful annoyance. *It's sort of nice not to be the one in the hot seat.*

"All right! Enough about me!" Ivy put her hands in the air. "I have some questions, too."

"Ask us anything," Olivia's mom challenged.

"What about Olivia's adoption?" Ivy asked eagerly.

Maybe Ivy will find out something I haven't been able to! Olivia thought.

"It was the happiest day of our lives," Olivia's dad said proudly.

"Did the agency tell you anything about our biological parents?" Ivy probed.

"No." Olivia's mom shrugged. "All they knew was what was written on the note that accompanied the baby: Olivia's name and her date of birth." A strange expression flickered briefly across Ivy's eyes.

"Must be just like the note in your own file," Olivia's mom guessed.

Ivy shook her head. "I don't have a note. I don't even have a file!"

Mrs. Abbott's face flushed with sympathy, and before Olivia knew it, her mom was rushing around the table to give Ivy a hug. To Olivia's surprise, Ivy didn't stiffen. In fact, she actually seemed comforted by it. Of course, Olivia's mom was a master of the art of hugging.

"I feel like I have a whole new daughter," Olivia's mom declared proudly as she began clearing the table a little while later. She beamed at Ivy. "I can't wait to see more of Olivia's other half."

Olivia watched for Ivy's reaction, half expecting her sister to look like a deer caught in headlights. Olivia loved her parents, but they could be superoverbearing sometimes.

Ivy looked genuinely touched though. "That sounds killer." She grinned.

The next thing Olivia knew, her father had a mountain of photo albums in his arms.

"Please, no," Olivia whined. "Ivy doesn't want

to see pictures. Do you, Ivy?"

"Wait until you see Olivia dressed as a green kangaroo in her kindergarten play. She was so *cute*!" her mom squealed.

"As a matter of fact," said Ivy, shooting Olivia a devilish grin as she followed Mr. Abbott into the living room, "I *would* like to see that."

Three photo albums and hundreds of embarrassing photos later, Olivia was pretty much at the end of her rope. To her relief, a car horn sounded outside.

Olivia leaped to her feet and looked out the living room window. "Ivy's dad's here," she said. "Time to go!"

"Aw," Ivy teased from where she was sandwiched between Olivia's parents on the couch. "But we're just getting started."

"Here's Olivia with spaghetti in her hair," her mom said.

"Sorry," Olivia said firmly, pulling her sister to her feet. "Show's over."

Ivy grinned. "Thank you so much for dinner, Mr. and Mrs. Abbott," she said.

"Call me Steve," Olivia's father said.

"And I'm Audrey," said Olivia's mother. "Why don't you invite your father in for a cup of coffee, Ivy?"

"I can't tonight," Ivy said apologetically. "I still have some homework to finish."

"Well," Olivia's mom said, "tell him we can't wait to meet him."

Olivia walked Ivy to the door.

"That wasn't bad at all," Ivy said in a low voice as she slipped into her jacket.

"You don't think so?" Olivia demanded. "Okay, next time we'll look at pictures of *you* drooling and wearing embarrassing clothes!"

Ivy laughed. "I'll see you in the morning at school," she said, giving Olivia a hug. "I bet nobody even reads the piece about us in the school paper."

"Probably not." Olivia shrugged. "But I'm still glad we told our parents."

"Me, too," Ivy agreed.

After Olivia had closed the door, her mom appeared and peered out through one of the glass panes.

"It must be hard," Audrey Abbott said

thoughtfully as Ivy climbed into her father's car, "with only one parent."

Olivia had never really thought about that. She gave her mom a hug. "I'm glad Ivy finally got to meet you," she whispered.

Over her mom's shoulder, Olivia saw her dad emerge from the living room.

"Nice girl, Ivy," he said matter-of-factly, "but who died?"

Olivia rolled her eyes and started to explain, *again*.

CHAPTER 3

Standing on the front steps of Franklin Grove Middle School, Ivy flipped open her fuzzy black spider watch and tapped it with a black fingernail. If it was really 8:10 on Wednesday morning, where were all the people? The steps should have been packed. *What if my watch is wrong and I'm late for class?* she thought.

As Ivy rushed toward the huge oak doors, she could hear a commotion inside. Stepping out of the cold December sunshine, she found herself engulfed in a chattering crowd of people.

Looking around, Ivy realized she was at the end of a huge, disorganized line that led to the tables where the school newspaper was distributed.

A pimply sixth-grader, who was coming the other way, walked right into her, his eyes glued to the front page of the paper in his hands. "Sorry," he mumbled. Then, glancing up, his mouth dropped open. "It's you!" he cried. "Or is it her?" he added suspiciously.

Ivy looked down at the paper he was holding and saw the towering headline, LONG-LOST TWINS FIND EACH OTHER! over huge, side-by-side photographs of Ivy and Olivia's faces. *So much for no one reading the article,* she thought with a grimace.

She put her head down, letting a curtain of dark hair conceal her face, and started elbowing her way through the crowd. Being the center of attention was hazardous to Ivy's health; it was like lying out in a bikini without any sunblock.

Luckily Ivy succeeded in plunging through the fray without anybody else recognizing her. Emerging at the edge of the crowd, she noticed another throng of people squeezing into a classroom up ahead. She skulked over and, balancing on the tips of her steel-toed boots, peered over everyone's heads.

Olivia was trapped in front of the whiteboard, still in her coat. She was flanked by Toby Decker, who had written the article for the school paper, and her friend Camilla Edmunson who was wearing a blue hoodie that said THE PAST WAS THE FUTURE on it. Camilla was seriously into sci-fi.

People were shouting questions.

"Can you read each other's minds?"

"Were you surgically separated at birth?"

"Have you ever met the Olsen twins?"

Olivia was trying to answer, but people kept interrupting.

"Did you always know you had a twin?" a girl in a red beret shouted.

Sort of, Ivy thought. Looking back, she had always felt like something was missing in her life, but she had never known what it was until the day she found Olivia.

In the middle of the classroom, greasy-haired Garrick Stephens, probably the lamest vampire in the whole school, got up on top of a desk. "Does anybody have any questions about when I climbed out of a coffin during a funeral?" he called. Garrick and his boneheaded friends—aka the Beasts—had recently sparked a witch hunt on national TV that had almost revealed the existence of vampires. Now he was clearly jealous that someone else was getting all the attention.

Somebody threw an eraser at his head, and he lost his balance and fell off the desk. Ivy couldn't keep from laughing, and a girl in front of her looked around and gasped.

"It's Ivy! The twin!" she gasped.

The words "Ivy" and "twin" rippled through the crowd. People turned their heads to look.

Uh-oh, thought Ivy.

"When one of you gets hurt, does the other one feel it?"

"Why don't you have the same color eyes?"

"Do you have any matching birthmarks?"

Soon everyone was shouting and talking and crowding around Ivy as well as Olivia. Instead of attempting to answer anyone's question, Ivy focused on trying not to fall over in the stampede.

Suddenly an earsplitting whistle rang out. Immediately, the crowd hushed. At the front of the room, Camilla was standing with one hand in the air authoritatively, the other to her lips. She looked like a traffic cop.

"Everyone stand still!" she commanded. Then Camilla jumped off the desk and pushed through the crowd. Grabbing Ivy's hand, she dragged her back to stand next to Olivia.

The sisters exchanged nervous looks. "You said nobody was going to read the article!" Ivy whispered.

"Oops." Olivia shrugged.

The room lit up with flashes from camera phones as people took pictures of the sisters side by side. "Ivy and Olivia can only answer one question at a time!" Camilla announced. "If you have a question, raise your hand." Scores of hands shot into the air.

Camilla was about to choose one, when a familiar high-pitched voice screeched, "Get out of my way!" The crowd parted, and Charlotte Brown—neighbor, nemesis, and cheerleading captain—shoved her way to the front. She looked from Ivy to Olivia with narrowed eyes. As her sidekicks, Katie and Allison, appeared behind her, she nodded.

"This explains a lot," Charlotte told her

friends, as if Ivy and Olivia couldn't hear her from five feet away.

Then Charlotte plastered an insincere look of sympathy on her face. "Don't worry, Olivia," she said loudly, "the cheerleading squad will stand by you no matter what."

All at once, Ivy's embarrassment gave way to annoyance. She trained her death squint on Charlotte Brown and was about to unleash an acid comeback when the bell rang.

Charlotte spun on her heel and headed for the door, her minions in tow. The rest of the crowd also started pouring out of the room.

Toby Decker, clearly delighted with the attention his story was receiving, patted Olivia and Ivy encouragingly on their backs as he squeezed past.

"Maybe we shouldn't have told anyone," Ivy said under her breath to her sister.

Olivia nodded and then grinned. "But, since we did, maybe we should have worn matching outfits!"

As she made her way among the tables at lunch, people Olivia didn't even know kept inviting her to sit with them. Luckily, she spotted Ivy's pale hand waving at her from a table near the window, where she was hiding behind Brendan. Olivia hurried over.

"Craziness!" Olivia sang, setting down her tray across from her sister.

"Brendan has heard that somebody is selling pictures of us on eBay," Ivy said wryly.

"Bidding's already up to ten bucks," Brendan announced.

Ivy's best friend, Sophia, put her tray down next to Ivy's, her camera hanging around her neck. "Ten bucks for what?" she asked.

"Somebody's selling pictures of Ivy and me on eBay," Olivia told her.

Sophia looked embarrassed.

Ivy stared at her in disbelief. "Please tell me you did not post pictures of us on eBay, Sophia."

"Sorry." Sophia gulped guiltily.

"Wow," Olivia teased. "Sold out by your own best friend!"

"I was going to split the money with you!" Sophia offered desperately.

"Oh," Ivy said, her face relaxing into a grin.

"That's okay, then!"

They all laughed, but a second later, Olivia realized she was the only one still chuckling. Her sister's eyes were fixed over her shoulder.

"Hi, Vera," Ivy said cautiously.

Olivia turned to find a Goth girl with a streak of white hair standing behind her. She knew Vera from the All Hallows' Ball committee meetings, where Olivia had impersonated Ivy.

"Last time I checked," Vera said, with a pointed glance at Olivia, "oil and water don't mix." Then she stuck her nose in the air and stalked off.

"What was that about?" Olivia asked when Vera was out of earshot.

Ivy lowered her voice. "Some vampires are a little . . . extreme in their views about mixing with bunnies—humans, I mean."

"But why?" Olivia wanted to know. "Aren't *we* supposed to be scared of *you*?"

"Not really," answered Sophia. "Your kind has a habit of breaking out the wooden stake first and asking questions later."

Ivy rolled her eyes. "As if that's happened this century."

"Either way," Brendan said diplomatically, "it's hard to have relationships with nonvamps when you're bound by a strict code of secrecy and have a weird diet."

"True," Ivy admitted. "It's easier with you because you know," she added to Olivia.

"Could that be why our parents split us up?" Olivia wondered aloud. She and her sister had been trying to figure out how a vampire and a human could be twins—and why their parents had separated them—for almost the whole time they'd known each other. "Maybe they were worried that if a vampire and a human grew up together, the vampire secret wouldn't be safe?" Olivia suggested.

Ivy grimaced. "Well, I certainly proved them right." She sighed. She'd broken the First Law of the Night by telling Olivia the truth about vampires, when bad scratches on her arm had healed before Olivia's eyes.

"You know I'd never tell," Olivia reassured her.

"Yes, and luckily," said Ivy, "no one beyond this table knows that you know, except for my dad, and he would never tell."

A question sprang into Olivia's mind. "But aren't all your friends going to guess that I know now, since it's out that we're sisters?"

Ivy stopped mid-sip of pink lemonade. "How come none of us thought of that?" she said to Sophia and Brendan.

The two of them shrugged worriedly in response.

Ivy bent to lightly bang her head against the table. "We're so dead," she said. "By the end of the day, every vamp in Franklin Grove is going to know we're sisters, and everyone's going to guess there's been a violation of the First Law."

"I suppose we could just deny it," Olivia whispered.

"Our community doesn't let things go that easily," Brendan said.

Ivy nodded in agreement. "We have no choice. We'll have to show everyone that you have a *right* to know."

"But how?" Sophia asked.

"By proving that one of our parents was a vampire, so Olivia's at least *part* vampire, too."

Olivia got goosebumps. It was weird to think of

vampire blood coursing through her veins. *Maybe I should try eating more steak,* she thought, but the idea made her stomach turn.

"The problem," Brendan said, "is that most people don't think it's possible for a human and a vamp to have normal kids."

"Well, they're wrong," Ivy said flatly. She turned to Olivia. "If we can locate our biological parents," she said, "and prove without a doubt that one of them was a vampire, then no one will be able to object to your knowing the secret."

"I'm game," Olivia said immediately. She'd give up her poms to know the truth about their parents anyway. "But what can we do? We already tried the adoption agency route, and that was a dead end."

"What about the VVV?" Sophia suggested.

"The what?" Olivia asked.

"The Vorld Vide Veb," Sophia said, sounding like the bloodsucking bride in an old vampire movie.

Olivia's jaw dropped. "Don't tell me vampires have their own Internet!"

"It was a vampire who *invented* the Internet,"

Brendan told her with a grin.

"You could try searching references to human-vampire relationships," Sophia suggested.

"And we should definitely look up Owl Creek, where we were born," Ivy added. "Olivia, can you come to my house after school? Then we can go online."

"Sure," Olivia agreed. "Maybe we can even find out something about what happens when vampires— Ow!" She broke off as somebody kicked her hard under the table.

"Hello, Camilla," Sophia said brightly, fixing her eyes on Olivia with a meaningful stare.

Olivia turned as Camilla sank down on the bench next to her, laying her thick, dog-eared paperback next to Olivia's tray.

"Hi," Camilla greeted everyone. "How are the star twins of Franklin Grove?"

"Awesome," Olivia blurted, while Ivy croaked, "Killer."

"How about you?" Olivia asked Camilla, with a sheepish smile as she reached under the table to rub her aching ankle. *Now* that *was close!* she thought.

CHAPTER 4

Ten minutes into last period, as Mr. Strain was going over the procedure for the cheek-cell experiment, Ivy glanced down at the piece of paper that she and Olivia had been passing back and forth since the beginning of class. It had started when Ivy had jotted down one possible theory concerning their parents. Olivia's latest pink-ink-penned theory was about halfway down.

THEORY 14: Mom bites Dad, feels guilty, runs off with kids, can't hack single parenthood???

Ivy tapped her pen thoughtfully against her lips. Glancing up, she caught Vera shooting her a mean look. Ivy returned her stare, and Vera angrily whispered the word "traitor" right at her. Ivy rolled her eyes and scribbled, *Vera should go eat some garlic!*

Olivia smiled when she read it, looked in Vera's direction, and then wrote, *Just ignore her!*

Mr. Strain came around to hand out materials, and Ivy covered the page with her book so he wouldn't see it. "I read the article in today's *Scribe,*" he said with a smile as he held out a tongue depressor for their experiment. "As twins, your cells should be nearly identical."

If so, then Olivia must *have some vamp in her,* thought Ivy. "Here's hoping," she said aloud.

"I keep meaning to ask," Olivia whispered once their teacher had moved on, "what are you doing this Saturday? My mom wants you to come over for lunch."

"Okay," Ivy said as she filled out their lab sheet.

Olivia sighed. "Then she wants to take the two of us shopping."

Ivy stopped writing. "I think that's the first time I've ever heard you sound unhappy about shopping," she pointed out.

"My mom is going completely overboard," Olivia explained. "After you left last night, she started researching Goth cookbooks, and got excited about some recipes she found."

"Really?" Ivy grinned. "Like what?"

"Blackberry blood soufflé," Olivia said, looking like just thinking about it made her want to puke.

"That does sound delicious," Ivy admitted.

"Gross," Olivia said under her breath.

"I hope that you will all discover something about your own genetics today," Mr. Strain told the class. "You may now begin."

As Olivia scraped the inside of her cheek, Ivy twirled her emerald ring around its chain. Their matching rings were the only things either of them had from their biological parents. While Olivia got to work on making their slide, Ivy took the chain from around her neck, and examined the ring thoughtfully. The emerald, a rich green, was set in a platinum band, which was covered with etchings in yellow gold that looked like rivers on Earth as seen from outer space.

As Olivia delicately pressed the two glass slides together, her ring sparkled up at Ivy.

Maybe the rings are some sort of clue, Ivy thought.

Ivy pulled the microscope over and slid her ring under the lens. Bringing it into focus, she followed the etchings with her eye, turning the ring slowly. Maybe she'd find something written there, between the tiny rivers.

Something caught her eye as she rotated the ring, but it wasn't on the band. It was actually in the emerald: a tiny blurry shape that looked like it was floating in the field of bright green.

"What is it?" Olivia whispered. "Let me see!"

"I don't know," Ivy said softly. "Probably just a flaw in the stone." She kept trying to adjust the position of the ring and the microscope's focus, but she couldn't make the blob out clearly.

Her sister poked her impatiently. Ivy pulled the ring out from under the microscope and held it up. She squinted, trying to see whatever it was with her naked eye, but she couldn't.

She turned the ring over. When she brought it right up to her nose, she could just barely make something out. She brushed one finger lightly over the exposed underside of the stone and felt tiny marks.

There's something carved on the bottom of the emerald! Ivy realized.

"What do you see?" Olivia asked eagerly.

Without answering, Ivy quickly put the ring back under the microscope lens, upside down this time. She turned the knob to refocus the microscope until . . .

She could see a tiny symbol, clear as night: it was the shape of an eye, with a *V* inside it.

"I can tell that you see something!" Olivia whispered urgently. Shoving Ivy over, she held her ponytail out of her way with one hand as she looked into the eyepiece.

"A symbol!" Olivia squealed as Ivy carefully drew the insignia in her notebook.

"Something wrong, ladies?" Mr. Strain called.

Olivia looked up. "Sorry, Mr. Strain," she said, smiling. "It's just that there's more to my . . . cheek than I ever realized!"

Ivy took her ring out from under the lens. Olivia replaced it with her own and bent back down over the eyepiece.

"Does yours have the same mark?" Ivy whispered.

Olivia nodded excitedly. "What do you think it is?"

"A jeweler's mark, maybe?" Ivy guessed.

Olivia looked up at her quizzically.

"Maybe the jeweler put this tiny symbol into his work," Ivy went on quietly, "the way a painter signs a painting. We might be able to use this mark to find the person who made the rings or cut the stones."

Olivia's eyes flickered as she caught on. "And that person might have a record of our parents' names!"

"I'm pretty sure that it's a vamp jeweler," Ivy said, taking a turn to look through the microscope at Olivia's ring. "I can tell from the symbol. Vamp businesses often hide tiny marks in their signs and logos and stuff to identify themselves as vampiric. They don't always use a *V*, but they often do."

Mr. Strain appeared in front of their desk. "That does not look like a cheek slide," he said sternly.

"We were just fooling around," Olivia said with a panicked glance at Ivy.

41

"Right," Ivy agreed. "We were being . . . ha ha . . . cheeky." Olivia giggled nervously as she returned her ring to her finger.

★ 🦇 ★

Ivy didn't have a chance to talk to Olivia again until they were heading home.

"Maybe we'll find out that our biological mother is a master jeweler!" Ivy said a few blocks from her house, her hands jammed in her pockets to protect them from the cold. "Maybe she made our rings herself."

"That would be cool," agreed Olivia.

Just then, Ivy's cell phone rang. "Dad," she announced, glancing at the caller ID display and flipping open the phone.

"Hello, Ivy," her father's smooth voice intoned. "Will you be joining me for dinner tonight? I am preparing hemoglobin stew with parsnips."

"Hi, Dad," Ivy said. "I'm glad you called. Olivia's coming over this afternoon to, uh . . ." Olivia mimed reading a book and taking notes. "Do some research," Ivy finished. "She's dying to meet you."

There was a long silence on the other end of the phone. "It is fine for Olivia to come over, but I am afraid I must leave for an appointment with a client," her father said at last.

"Can't you change it?" Ivy pleaded.

"No," her father said simply. "My regrets," he finished and hung up.

Ivy sighed, her warm breath forming a frosty cloud in the air. "The good news," she told her sister, "is that the computer will be free." She kicked a rock into a pile of frozen leaves. "The bad news is that my dad won't be there." She couldn't help feeling disappointed. *Why isn't my dad more eager to meet my twin sister?* she thought.

"That's okay," Olivia said, swinging her book bag onto her other shoulder and putting her arm through Ivy's. "We'll cross paths one of these days."

"He's already two hundred years old," Ivy said with a roll of her eyes. "'One of these days' could be two decades from now!"

Olivia had been to Ivy's a handful of times before, but the mansion at the top of the hill still blew her away. From the outside, the place looked like something out of a Civil War epic—or an old black-and-white vampire movie.

The inside was just as glamorous. She'd seen Ivy's basement crypt bedroom with its huge closet. And she'd helped to decorate the gothic third floor ballroom for the All Hallows' Ball, so she wasn't expecting Mr. Vega's study to be a pile of old decorating magazines on top of a banged-up filing cabinet. Still, Olivia couldn't keep from being impressed when Ivy opened the door to the study on the second floor.

All four walls were lined with bookshelves. There was a huge mahogany desk crowned by a flat-screen computer monitor, and across the room was an enormous globe in the middle of a rug that looked like a starry sky. Next to it, on top of a wide pedestal, stood a gray model with tiny paintings on the walls.

And *then* Olivia looked up, and realized that the dark-wood bookshelves lining the walls stretched up for another story, and there was a narrow walkway—like a balcony—to enable browsing up there.

This place is awesome! she thought.

Ivy dragged a second high-backed black-lacquer chair behind the desk and motioned for Olivia to sit beside her as she powered up her dad's computer.

The screen lit up with a black-and-white photograph of Ivy in profile, looking thoughtful, the outline of tree branches against a sunset sky behind her.

"I wish my father would change his background," Ivy said with a sigh.

"But that's such a good picture of you!" Olivia exclaimed.

"Look at my nose," her sister scoffed. "It's huge."

"Hey," Olivia countered with mock offense. "You better be careful what you say about our nose!"

Ivy grinned. "Are you ready for the Vorld Vide Veb?" she asked.

Olivia nodded and Ivy clicked on an icon of a moon in the corner, and the screen went black, except for three big Gothic letters in the center:

V V V

"Can anyone access this?" Olivia asked.

Ivy shook her head. "Your computer needs a special chip just to get this far."

Ivy carefully started clicking on the letters: the upper left tip of the first **V**, then the bottom of the **V**, then the place where the upper right tip of the first **V** met the upper left of the second **V**.

"What are you doing?" Olivia asked.

"You'll see," said Ivy. Her seventh click, on the upper right-hand corner of the third *V*, prompted her for a user name and password.

After Ivy had typed them in, a question appeared on the screen: *How do you like your coffee?*

"Wow!" Olivia remarked, impressed by the site's security. "They really know a lot about you."

Ivy chuckled. "It's a riddle," she explained. "It's different every time. Want to guess?"

Olivia read the question again. "With sweetener?" she tried.

"You are such a bunny," Ivy teased. Then she typed in the letters *B-L-A-C-K*.

The screen flashed, and a search engine called Moonlight appeared on screen. *Illuminate the darkness*, it said underneath the entry box.

"Is there *anything* vampires don't have their own secret version of?" Olivia asked in amazement.

"A cruise liner," Ivy replied as she typed in JEWELERS' MARKS. "Vamps don't really like water."

There were 272,000 results, and the first one was the Web site for the Vampire Jewelers Association (VJA), which offered *one of the most comprehensive registries of jewelers' marks in the underworld.* Ivy clicked on the link, and seconds later she and Olivia were scanning the marks of thousands of vampire jewelers. Some looked like cat's whiskers, some like tiny coffins, lots incorporated a *V* in some way—but none looked like the symbol on their rings.

After the VJA site, they tried the listing on the Antique Jewelry Guild site. Eventually, there was only one page of symbols left to see. Ivy took a deep breath and clicked.

The page filled with marks.

Not one even vaguely resembles the insignia on our emeralds, Olivia thought disappointedly.

Ivy sighed. "If it's not a jeweler's mark, it could be anything."

Determined to remain upbeat, Olivia suggested they try searching for something else. Ivy went back to the Moonlight page.

"Type in 'human-vampire relationships,'" Olivia instructed, so Ivy did.

Results flooded the screen:

Crossbreed Born with Four Heads

Mixed Offspring Eats Self to Death

Monstrous Hybrid Stalks Sewers

Bat Baby Terrorizes Hospital!

"W-what is all this?" Olivia stammered.

"Tabloid headlines," Ivy answered wearily. "Vamp rags are full of over-the-top stories about what happens when a human and a vamp try to have a baby."

"They have bat babies?" Olivia said in disbelief.

"Of course not," Ivy dismissed. "Here's something that doesn't sound insane," she went on, running her cursor over a link near the bottom of the screen: "Genetic Barriers to Crossbreeding: A Scientific Study." Ivy clicked and ended up on the Web site for something called the *Vampiric Journal of Biomedical Sciences*.

Olivia read the summary of the article aloud. "'This V-Gen-sponsored study compares the genetic makeup of vampires and humans in order to objectively assess the possibility of successfully bearing healthy crossbreed offspring. Findings suggest that the significant differences between vampire and human DNA amount to an insurmountable obstacle of a magnitude similar to that found between canines and felines.'" Olivia looked at her sister. "Is it just me, or does this say that you and me are about as likely as puppies born to a cat and dog?"

Ivy sighed. "That's what it says," she agreed. "But we're obviously *not* impossible," she went on. "I mean, we exist and we're sisters!" She scanned the screen and then gasped suddenly. "No way!"

"What?" Olivia asked.

"This article was written by Marc Daniels. That's Brendan's father's name!"

"Are you sure?" Olivia asked, peering at the screen. She pointed to a line at the end of the research report. "Is Brendan's dad head researcher of V-Gen?"

Ivy shrugged. She quickly went back to the main search page and typed in V-Gen. The top result said, *V-GEN—a leading vampire pharmaceutical company based in Franklin Grove.*

Olivia and Ivy both stared at the screen for a long moment, taking in the indisputable fact that Brendan's father was the same Marc Daniels who had written the article.

"We have to talk to him," Olivia said at last.

Ivy bit her lip. "Judging from his research, he's not really on our side," she said.

"Maybe we can change his mind," Olivia proposed.

"Even if we could, Olivia," responded Ivy, "I can't talk to my boyfriend's father about how babies are made."

"Sure you can!" Olivia laughed. "He'll understand. Come on, Ivy. We have to get answers! Ask Brendan tomorrow if he'll introduce us to his dad. *Please.*"

"I am not going to bring this up at school," Ivy declared decisively, and Olivia's heart sank. Then Ivy added quietly, "I have a date with Brendan on Friday. I'll ask him then."

Olivia clapped her hands. "Talking to a vampire geneticist about how we're twins is going to be way more interesting than cheek cells!"

★ 🦇 ★

At school on Thursday, the whole twin frenzy was even more intense than it had been the day before. After fourth period, Ivy saw a sixth-grader wearing a baby tee that said, I WANNA GOTH TWIN.

I'm a fad! Ivy thought, horrified. If she could have dug a hole, climbed into her coffin, and lowered herself into the ground, she would have. She felt so ill by the end of the day that she canceled after-school plans with Olivia—they had been going to make a list of questions for Mr. Daniels—and went straight home.

★ 🦇 ★

That night, Ivy was in her pajamas, reading before bed, when she heard footsteps descending the basement stairs. She watched as her father came slowly into view.

"You cleaned your room," he said approvingly. That's when Ivy knew something was wrong, because, if anything, the basement was an even bigger mess than usual. She sat up and closed her book.

"Ivy," he said when he reached the bottom of the stairs, "I need to speak with you.

"Do you recall the hotel job I mentioned several weeks ago?" he asked.

"You mean the one in Europe?" Ivy said. Her father nodded in confirmation. A chain of vampire-funded hotels had wanted to hire him to be their interior designer. It was a really good job, but he had said he didn't want to leave Franklin Grove.

"I've accepted the job," Mr. Vega announced.

Ivy blinked. "I thought you already said no."

"I did." He cleared his throat. "But now they have made me an offer that I cannot refuse."

"What?" gasped Ivy.

"I have to." He paused. "I would not be able to live with myself if I didn't take the job. I start in about three weeks."

A chill came over Ivy. She pulled the sleeves of

her pajamas down around her wrists. "So you're going to Europe?"

Her father nodded apologetically.

"But how am I supposed to stay in Franklin Grove if you go to Europe?" she asked.

He pulled a black handkerchief from his pocket and wrung it absentmindedly. "You won't," he said, a pained look in his eyes. "You'll be coming with me."

Ivy's heart seized. "You're taking me out of school?"

"There is a very good academy for girls like you in Luxembourg," her father answered in a weary voice.

"I can't!" she cried in horror, pulling a black cat pillow in front of her.

"We must," her father said.

"All my friends are here!" Ivy pleaded.

"You will make new friends."

"What about Olivia?"

Her father studied his hands. "I'm sorry," he said quietly.

Ivy could feel tears starting to slide down her cheeks. "Why are you doing this?" she quavered.

"Ivy, I am taking this job for you," he said gently. "You will understand one day, when you are a parent."

Without saying anything more, her father started to walk away. He turned to look back at her solemnly before climbing the stairs. "We'll be moving during your winter break. I know how hard this will be for you, Ivy. But try to think of it as a new adventure. For both of us," he finished. Then he was gone.

Ivy was stunned. *How can I leave Franklin Grove? How can I leave Olivia and my friends? None of this makes sense!*

Ivy instinctively reached for the phone, but then realized that it was too late to call anyone. She buried her face in her cat pillow and stayed that way, thinking, unable to fall asleep for hours.

CHAPTER 5

When Olivia walked out of homeroom on Friday morning, Ivy and Sophia were waiting for her. Ivy's voice sounded weakly from behind her dark hair. "Can you come to the science hall bathroom for a second?"

Poor Ivy, Olivia thought. *All the attention is really getting to her.*

A moment later, the three of them were alone in the empty bathroom. Ivy pushed her hair out of her face, and Olivia saw that her eyes were red from crying.

"What happened?" Olivia and Sophia said at the same time.

Ivy smiled for a moment. Then her face crumpled like one of those buildings that gets blown up to make way for a parking lot. "I'm moving to Europe," she sobbed.

Sophia looked sideways at Olivia. "Did she just say she's 'moody like syrup'?"

"I th-think she s-said she's moving to Europe," Olivia stammered.

"What?" Sophia cried.

Ivy nodded in confirmation.

Olivia put out her hand, and Ivy grabbed it as if it were a lifeline. Sophia grasped Ivy's other hand.

"It's okay," Olivia cooed, trying to keep her head.

"When is this happening?" Sophia asked.

It took Ivy three attempts before she could get the answer out. "Winter break," she sobbed.

"But that's barely three weeks away!" exclaimed Sophia, and Olivia's heart plunged into her sneakers.

"Why?" Olivia asked, her voice tight.

Ivy couldn't answer. Not letting go of her hand, Olivia inched over to the dispenser on the wall and pulled out some paper towels. She gave them to Ivy, who took them and blew her nose.

Ivy took a deep breath. "My dad took a job in *Luxembourg*," she explained. She said "Luxembourg" like it was the North Pole.

Olivia shook her head slowly, the reflection in the bathroom mirror blurring as her own eyes filled with tears. "But you can't go," she said. "I only just found you!"

"You can't go," Sophia repeated. "You're my best friend!"

"I have to," Ivy said, and now they were all sobbing. The three of them flung their arms around one another and bawled.

When Olivia finally pulled away, Sophia and Ivy's faces were both muddy with black mascara. She couldn't help laughing. "You two look like raccoons."

"So do you," Sophia laugh-cried. Olivia looked in the mirror and saw that Sophia was right. Their Goth makeup had rubbed off on her face.

Olivia washed her face and was starting to reapply some blush when something else occurred to her. "Have you told Brendan yet?" she asked Ivy.

Ivy didn't say anything, but suddenly her skin started turning a color Olivia had never seen before. It was pink, as if she was blushing.

"She's going to faint!" Sophia cried.

Ivy's eyelids fluttered and she slumped against the sink. Olivia rushed to hold her up. Sophia turned on the tap and threw a handful of water in Ivy's face. Nothing happened, so Sophia tried again.

"Stop!" Ivy spluttered. "Stop it!" She stood on her own two feet and glared at Sophia. "What are you trying to do—drown me?"

"You fainted," Sophia said apologetically.

"What? I never faint!" Ivy said in disbelief.

"Olivia asked you about Brendan," Sophia explained gently.

Ivy blinked. Then she let out a tortured sigh. "Oh, yeah," she whispered.

"I thought people were supposed to turn white before they faint," Olivia said.

"Not vamps." Sophia shook her head. "We blush."

Ivy started drying her face with a paper towel. "I hadn't even thought about Brendan," she said hoarsely. "I guess I just didn't *want* to think about it. Losing the two of you is bad enough."

Olivia set her jaw. She didn't want to start crying again.

"I'm going to the arcade with him tonight," Ivy went on forlornly. "I guess I'll have to tell him then."

Facing the mirror, side by side, the three of them silently went about cleaning themselves up. After giving Ivy a hug, Sophia left first, because she had to get a book from her locker before next period.

As Ivy finished reapplying her mascara, Olivia stared at the floor. "Do you think we should keep looking for the truth about our parents?" she asked.

"The fact that you know about vampires' existence isn't going to change when I'm gone," Ivy answered, though she only mouthed the word "vampires." "It's probably even more important to justify your knowing the secret now, since I won't be around to protect you."

Olivia nodded and a small smile found its way to her lips. Her sister was right—and anyway she wanted to know the truth about their parents.

"Can I come visit you?" Olivia asked in a small voice.

Ivy's reflection looked her in the eye. "You'd better." She spun around, and they hugged.

In unison, they swung their bags onto their shoulders and prepared to walk out. "Are you still coming over for lunch tomorrow?" said Olivia. "My mom's all excited to go shopping."

"Absolutely." Ivy grinned as she swung open the door and led Olivia into the bustling hallway. "I'm not gone yet."

★ 🦇 ★

Friday night, Ivy stood in the shadows near the doorway of the mall arcade, squeezed between the wall and the side of a hulking airplane cockpit game. From there she could watch Brendan undetected, as he stood waiting for her by the air hockey table across the room.

His broad shoulders were cloaked in a dark gray, military-style jacket over a bright ghoulgreen T-shirt. His curly black hair, still wet from the rain, glistened in the dim blue light of the arcade. He was drop-dead in every way. He tapped an air hockey panel on the edge of the table absentmindedly.

Their first date had been here, not so long ago. Brendan had surprised Ivy by challenging her to a running air hockey competition, and Ivy had never had so much fun in her life. As their relationship had grown, so had their tournament: the score now stood at Ivy 23, Brendan 22. They were always neck and neck. Ivy wanted to be neck and neck forever.

She had spent so many years pining over Brendan Daniels without having the nerve to speak to him, and now he was her boyfriend. *How am I going to leave him?* she thought, a sharp pain piercing her heart. But she knew she didn't have a choice.

Ivy was prepared for the possibility that tonight would be their final date. How could they stay together when an ocean was going to separate them?

Bracing herself, Ivy stepped out of the corner. Brendan spotted her right away. Bounding over, he kissed her on the cheek, grabbed her hand, and dragged her back to the air hockey table.

"I've been waiting all week to take the headlines away from you!" he announced. He paused at the side of the table, spreading his hands in the air as if imagining the cover of the next *Scribe*: "Daniels Beats Vega in Air Hockey Hullabaloo!" Brendan reached into his pocket and took out some tokens. He bent down to put them into the slot, but Ivy forced herself to put her hand on top of his at the last moment.

"Wait," she said quietly.

Brendan stopped and looked at her. Ivy entwined her pale fingers in his own and led him away from the table, deeper into the arcade. Finally they stood in the corner near the retro games, where it was quieter.

"Brendan"—her voice shook—"my dad has got a new job."

"That's great!" he responded, but his smile started to fade as his eyes searched her face. "Isn't it?"

"It's in Europe," Ivy answered. She took a deep breath. "We're moving in three weeks."

Something dark flickered in Brendan's eyes. Suddenly, he looked down at their hands. "You're leaving?" he said without looking up.

Ivy nodded. He shook his head without meeting her eye.

This is the end, thought Ivy.

Then Brendan started to stroke Ivy's fingers thoughtfully. Suddenly he looked up at her with determination. "Distance doesn't matter," he declared.

"Brendan . . ." she began, feeling for some reason like she should argue.

"It doesn't," he said forcefully. "We can call and e-mail and IM."

"There's a time difference," Ivy cautioned.

"I've always wanted to visit Europe," Brendan said, unfazed. "Everyone says it sucks."

"You'd visit me?" Ivy quavered. Brendan looked into her eyes, put his arms around her, and pulled her close.

Ivy buried her face in his chest. "I don't know how I'm going to say good-bye to you," she whispered.

"You don't have to," Brendan said into her hair. Ivy looked up at him, and her heart fluttered.

He smiled down at her easily. "I think we need a new game," Brendan said, looking around, "one that we can play when we're apart and then compare scores." Suddenly his eyes focused across the room, and his eyebrows shot up. "Skee-Ball!"

He started pulling her across the arcade, but Ivy hung back; somehow, it didn't seem right to play a game. "I don't know," she murmured.

"Ivy," Brendan said firmly, "we only have three weeks. It's okay to be sad when you're gone. But I don't want to spend time being sad while you're still here."

You're right, Ivy thought. *And you're mine!* She smiled, and together they raced across the arcade.

"I'm warning you," Brendan told her, "my high score is unbeatable!"

A few minutes later, Ivy had sunk her second five-hundred-point bull's-eye in a row. "She's . . . killing . . . me," Brendan croaked. He slumped onto the empty next lane, his eyes closed and his tongue lolling out of his mouth.

Grinning, Ivy prepared for her next throw. She was just releasing the ball when Brendan sprang up and hissed at her, baring imaginary fangs. The wooden ball careened wildly up the slope, shot up against the top of the cage, and bounced out of the alley.

"Brendan!" Ivy scolded.

The ball rolled onto the floor, and Ivy chased after it. For a moment she lost sight of it among people's legs, but then she spotted the ball as it collided with someone's black wingtip shoe with a hollow thump.

The man whose foot she'd hit leaned down and scooped up the ball. He held it out in front of him, staring at Ivy curiously. Underneath a gray wool overcoat, he was wearing a dark blue shirt. He wore round glasses, and he had wild, graying curly hair that emanated from his head in all directions. He looked like a maniacal genius.

"S-sorry," Ivy stammered.

The man dropped the ball into her hand.

"Dad!" Brendan exclaimed, coming over to join Ivy. "What are you doing here?"

Ivy turned to look at Brendan and then back at the man standing before her. She couldn't believe her luck. Not only was Brendan being more A positive about her move to Europe than she could ever have hoped but now she was getting to meet his father without even asking!

Brendan inched up to his dad. "I'm on a date," he murmured in a low voice.

Somehow, Ivy thought, *embarrassment makes him even more gorgeous.*

"Your mother asked me to tell you to be home in time for dinner," Mr. Daniels said haltingly. He glanced at Ivy again, then stared expectantly at Brendan.

"Dad, this is Ivy. Ivy, this is my dad," Brendan muttered.

Brendan's father extended his hand. "It is a great pleasure to meet you," he said, turning Ivy's hand over in his own curiously. He looked up at her with sparkling eyes. "I understand you have a twin sister?"

"Dad!" Brendan scolded. He looked at Ivy apologetically. "My dad's a geneticist."

"It's okay," Ivy said. *Mr. Daniels seems just as eager to talk to me as Olivia and I are to talk to him!* she thought excitedly. "Great to meet you, Mr. Daniels."

He peered into her eyes. "Any health problems

as a child?" he asked clinically.

Ivy thought about it. "No. I got a marble stuck in my ear once."

"Are you allergic to garlic?" he asked.

"Of course," Ivy answered.

"Inconceivable," Mr. Daniels muttered to himself.

"Sorry to interrupt," Brendan said, sounding annoyed, "but did I mention that Ivy and I are on a *date*?" He grabbed his father's arm and dragged him away.

A minute later, Brendan reappeared, unaccompanied, next to Ivy at the Skee-Ball game.

"Sorry about that," he said sheepishly as Ivy handed him a ball. "Ever since he heard about you and Olivia, he's been desperate to meet you."

Brendan shot the ball, and it bounced into the circle just outside the bull's-eye. "Four hundred points," he announced.

"You want to hear something deadly?" Ivy said, taking a ball. "I was actually going to ask if I could talk to your dad." She shot one hundred points and grimaced.

"How come?" Brendan asked.

"Olivia and I found a research study that he wrote about whether vamps and humans can have babies. We kind of wanted to ask him about that."

"Then you would actually be willing to come over to our house for lunch on Sunday?" Brendan said with a hint of relief. "My dad asked me to invite you and Olivia."

"That would be killer!" Ivy said.

"Maybe to you," remarked Brendan. "You don't have to listen to him talk about work all the time! But at least this way he can get all his scientific mumbo jumbo out in one dose, and you and Olivia can ask any questions you want."

"He doesn't know that Olivia knows about, you know, though, right?" Ivy said cryptically.

"Ivy," Brendan assured her, "I would never tell anyone your secrets. *Especially* my parents."

Smiling, Ivy picked up the ball and aimed for the bull's-eye. She'd invite Olivia to lunch with Brendan's family when she went to Olivia's house for lunch tomorrow. Ivy bowled the ball up the ramp, and it sailed into the five-hundred-point hole in the center. "Yes!" she cried.

Brendan sighed. "At least when you go," he said, "I can have the high-score record for North America back."

CHAPTER 6

Olivia skulked to answer the door on Saturday afternoon. Since finding out that Ivy was moving, her mom's Ivy-related plans had become way too intense. Olivia glared at her own makeup-whitened face in the foyer mirror before opening the door.

Ivy looked her up and down. "Don't you think it's a little risky to try and switch for lunch with your parents?" she whispered. "Besides, I would never wear black pants and black flats like that— it looks far too businesslike."

"I'm not trying to be you," Olivia seethed through clenched teeth. "My mom's making us all go Goth in your honor!"

Ivy started laughing. "If you think *I* look funny," Olivia huffed, "wait till you see my parents!"

She led Ivy to the dining room, where her mom had set the table. "Despite it being weeks ago, we're pretending it's Halloween," said Olivia glumly. Her mom had draped the table with a black tablecloth on which she'd ironed white appliqué skulls. In the center of the table was a candle, and there were cheesy napkins with jack-o'-lanterns on them from a costume party they'd had when Olivia was like six.

"Ivy's here," Olivia called in a loud voice.

Ivy looked around, clearly confused that Olivia's parents were nowhere to be seen.

Suddenly there was a creaking noise, and just outside the French doors that opened onto the patio, the basement cellar door was flung open. Out climbed Olivia's dad dressed in black leather pants, a dark purple button-down shirt, and a black tie with glow-in-the-dark eyeballs on it. His breath looked like clouds of smoke in the cold December air.

"Is your father wearing eyeliner?" Ivy whispered.

Olivia nodded, speechless with horror.

"Deadly to see you, Ivy," her father said haltingly as he opened the French doors and came in.

"Hi, Mr. Abbott." Ivy smiled. "Nice pants."

Suddenly a few notes of eerie classical music boomed through the house, so loud that Olivia and Ivy both put their hands to their ears. Somebody turned down the volume abruptly, and then smoke started pouring out of the cellar.

"Dry ice," Olivia's father said proudly.

A pale hand emerged, quivering, from the cellar. Then Olivia's mom floated up the steps in a shredded black dress and bunny ears that she'd spray-painted black. She was wearing heavy black makeup: eyeliner, mascara, lipstick—the works. She was even wearing gray blush, which made her look sort of dead.

"Welcome to the Abbott haunted house," Olivia said under her breath.

Her mom entered the dining room. "Greetings, Ivy!" she said dramatically—in a British accent for no apparent reason.

Ivy giggled and curtsied, which only made things worse.

They all sat down to lunch, and Olivia's mom proudly served up the Beef Ghoulash she'd made. It smelled really gross, so Olivia tried not to breathe through her nose at all. Her mom had made "blood" (tomato) soup specially for her, so she stuck to that and helped herself to the blackened blue potato salad.

"So, Ivy, Olivia tells us you live in quite a . . . pad?" Olivia's dad attempted. Olivia's mom shook her head disapprovingly at him.

"Quite a house?" he tried.

"One as nightmarish as you can do better than that, Steve," Olivia's mom challenged.

"Quite a . . . crypt?" he said tentatively.

Her mom nodded approvingly, and Olivia put her head in her hands.

Ivy grinned. "Our house is one of the oldest in Franklin Grove," she answered.

Olivia couldn't believe that her sister actually seemed to be enjoying herself. She decided to try and steer the conversation away from Goth-related topics, so that, just maybe, her parents would stop embarrassing her.

"You know, Ivy was once a cheerleader," Olivia said brightly.

"Really?" Olivia's mom asked eagerly, her regular perky self showing through for a moment.

Ivy nodded. "It's true," she confirmed. And as she told Mr. and Mrs. Abbott all about it, Olivia hoped she'd hit on the one subject her parents couldn't possibly turn Goth.

Olivia's dad cleared his throat. "Go on, Audrey," he said encouragingly. "Let your darkness shine!"

"Well, actually," Olivia's mom began, "when we were decorating today, a little Goth cheer happened to come into my head."

Olivia groaned. "Please, no!"

Ivy elbowed her sister and said, "I'd love to hear it."

Olivia shot her a death squint as her parents stood up and moved to the side of the table. Her mom struck some sort of zombie pose, her dad did the same, and Olivia wished the floor would open up and swallow her.

"We are Gothic. We are dark!" Olivia's mom

moved jerkily as she chanted and struck a new zombie pose when she stopped.

"We are Gothic in the park!" Mr. Abbott chimed in.

Olivia rolled her eyes. Then her parents started chanting together.

"See us brood and see us prowl. We will scare you with our growl! Grrr, grr, grr!"

Ivy clapped loudly. "I'd love to see Olivia and the squad do that one," she said, grinning.

Olivia's mom looked hopeful as she sat back down at the table.

"Maybe you could teach it to me later," Olivia said wearily.

After what seemed like hours, everybody finished eating and Olivia jumped to her feet. "I'll clear the table," she volunteered.

"I'll help," Ivy offered.

Olivia's mom started to protest, but Olivia said, "Have a seat, Elvira!"

"It's customary in Goth culture for the twin girls to clear the dishes," Ivy added with a smile.

"I guess we could get used to that," Olivia's mom responded, grinning at her husband.

Once they'd made it into the kitchen, Olivia set the plates down and turned to look at her sister. "Are you freaking out?" she blurted. "Because I'm freaking out!"

"No," Ivy answered. "Why?"

"You don't think this is strange behavior for parents?" Olivia demanded.

"Olivia, my father won't even meet you!" Ivy said. "At least your parents are trying. Besides, if you think you're embarrassed by your parents, you should have seen Brendan at the mall last night when his dad showed up."

Olivia put down the sponge. "You met Brendan's father?"

Ivy nodded. "He wants you and me to come over to their house for lunch tomorrow. Apparently, Mr. Daniels has been dying to talk to us. Can you come?"

"Sure!" Olivia said, rinsing a plate. "Do you really think he might be able to prove I have some vamp in me?"

Ivy glanced nervously toward the doorway to make sure no one was around. "You can't say

76

anything like that tomorrow at the Daniels',
Olivia. If Brendan's parents find out that I told
you, who knows what might happen?"

*How are we supposed to talk about anything with
Brendan's father,* Olivia thought, *if we're not
allowed to talk about anything?* At the same time,
she knew her sister was right.

Olivia was drying the last dish when she realized
she was dreading returning to the dining room,
where her parents were still posing as Goths.

"Would it be okay if I didn't go shopping with
you and my mom?" Olivia asked Ivy tentatively.

"*You* don't want to go *shopping*?" Ivy marveled.

"I can't take any more of my mom's weird-
ness," Olivia admitted. "I could stay here and do
more research on the Internet—like, looking up
twins in Owl Creek."

"Okay," Ivy agreed. "I've never had a mother
before. It'll suck to have one to myself for a whole
afternoon."

★ 🦇 ★

"Let's get manicures!" Olivia's mom said to Ivy
excitedly as they descended the escalator. There

was a new nail place called Cute-icles on the ground floor.

"Why not?" Ivy said gamely. "I've never had a manicure before."

"But you have such beautiful hands!" Audrey exclaimed as they stepped off the escalator.

Now this is what I need a mother for, Ivy thought as Audrey pulled her along enthusiastically.

"What color are you getting?" Audrey asked her, staring down at the tray of bottles.

Ivy looked at all the different colors. "I think I'll go for Midnight Maroon."

"That's what I was going to pick!" Olivia's mom squealed. "The girls in bridge club are going to be so shocked."

When they were done at the nail salon, they flitted from store to store, trying on funny earrings and stuff. At Spins Records, Audrey asked Ivy to play her "what the Goth kids are listening to," and then proceeded to seriously rock out at a listening station to the new Final Fangtasy album, doing a zombie dance in the aisle. *Now I know where Olivia gets her bubbliness from,* thought Ivy.

After that they went to Dungeon Clothing,

where Olivia's mom noticed Ivy admiring a top and made her try it on. Peeking out from behind the dressing room curtain, Ivy spied Audrey waiting for her to emerge. For a moment, she tried to pretend that she really was her mother. *This is what it's like,* she thought, *to go shopping with your mom.*

Ivy stepped out from behind the curtain and cleared her throat. Audrey sprang up from her seat and looked her up and down. "That looks deadly awesome!"

Ivy couldn't help smiling at Audrey's mangled speech. "You think so?" she said, turning around and looking herself over in the mirror. The top really was drop-dead—it was like a black spider-web stretched over a shimmery gray satin camisole—but it didn't seem to fit quite right.

Audrey held a finger up and rummaged through her purse. Finding some safety pins, she stood behind Ivy and took a handful of fabric. "Hold still," she said and popped two pins in.

It was as if the top was transformed by a magic spell before Ivy's eyes. It hung perfectly. "H-how did you do that?" Ivy stammered.

"Olivia says I'm a domestic goddess," Audrey replied proudly.

Moms totally suck! thought Ivy.

A little while later, she and Audrey were sharing a table in the food court.

"So tell me about your father," Audrey asked, sipping a Diet Coke daintily so she wouldn't smudge her latest application of Ivy's lipstick. Ivy put down her burger and stared at her plate. "Don't you get along with him?" Audrey pressed.

"I usually do," Ivy admitted. "I mean, I love him. He's always been amazing. But it's hard not to be mad at him lately."

"Why?"

"Because I don't want to move to Europe," Ivy answered glumly.

Audrey nodded sympathetically. "I remember when Steve told me he needed to move to Franklin Grove for work."

"What did you do?" Ivy asked.

"I cried," Audrey recalled. "And Olivia, well . . . she wouldn't come out of her room for a week. It was awful."

"Then what happened?" asked Ivy.

"Now I can't imagine living anywhere else," Audrey said, smiling. She reached out and put her hand on Ivy's. "You'll be all right," she said. "Nothing can break the bond you and Olivia share. Not even an ocean."

Ivy nodded bravely.

Suddenly Audrey glanced at her watch and her face fell. "Oh, my goodness, how time flies!"

As they drove out of the parking lot a little while later, she offered to take Ivy home. Ivy was about to accept when Audrey added brightly, "I could meet your father."

"I just remembered," Ivy improvised. "I promised Olivia before we left that I'd meet her back at your house . . . so that she could walk me home . . . for the exercise."

"You're sure I shouldn't just drive you?" Audrey said, clearly disappointed.

"Maybe another day," Ivy said as cheerily as she could.

★ 🦇 ★

Olivia was actually relieved to have an excuse to get out of the house. Just the sound of her mother's voice squealing "way deadly!" to Ivy upon their return from the mall made her want to scream.

"How'd your research into our parents go?" Ivy asked as they strolled past the cemetery on the way to Ivy's house.

"Pathetically," Olivia answered. "You know how many sets of twins there are from Owl Creek?"

"I can think of at least one," said Ivy.

"Three," Olivia said. "Aside from us, there's Eddie and Freddie, who now run a pizza parlor in Chicago, and a brother and sister figure skating Roller Derby team. Want to guess what the skaters call themselves?"

Ivy made a face. "I thought *we* were a strange pair."

"The Slippery Sliders," Olivia revealed.

Ivy groaned.

"I couldn't find any mention of us—or even a birth announcement for twin girls," Olivia lamented. *It's hard not to be discouraged when every path we explore leads nowhere,* she thought.

Ivy nodded sadly, almost like she could hear Olivia's thoughts. Then she stopped. "Did I show you the top your mom got me?"

When Olivia shook her head, Ivy reached into her knapsack and pulled out a low-cut, supercute spiderweb thingy. She held it up in front of her and batted her thick black eyelashes.

Olivia gaped. "My mom wouldn't let me out of the house in a shirt like that!"

"Well, she was like a vamp in a bloodbath today," Ivy said matter-of-factly. "You should have seen her doing the zombie in the middle of Spins."

Olivia covered her eyes with her hands. "I always thought my dad was the embarrassing one. Anyway," she continued, determined to be mature about it, "I'm glad you two had a good time."

Ivy nodded. Olivia looked at her. "Didn't you?"

"Of course," Ivy said quietly. "She was utterly great, and I . . . well, I kind of found out what it was like to have a mom." She kicked the pavement with the tip of her boot. "But Audrey's not my mom," she went on. "She's yours. You're really lucky, Olivia," she finished in a whisper.

Olivia felt tears spring to her eyes. *Yeah, I am,*

she thought. She wrapped Ivy's arm in her hands and, together, they climbed Ivy's long driveway in silence.

"Dad!" Ivy called, unlocking the enormous front door. "Olivia's here!" Her voice echoed through the stone corridors. "Dad?"

Olivia followed Ivy to the kitchen. There, on the stone counter, lay a note.

"'Darling,'" Ivy read aloud, "'I got your message, but I had to go out. Regards to your friend Olivia.'"

"'Your friend'?" Olivia repeated incredulously.

Ivy threw her bag on the countertop. "I can't believe it. He's purposely avoiding you because you're human!" she seethed. "Well, at least we can do some more investigating into our *real* parents on the VVV."

Olivia hadn't seen her sister so mad. She shook her head. "I think we've had enough of parents for one week," she said. "Why don't we have some fun? Call Sophia and see if she can come over."

A half hour later, the three of them were hanging out in the living room, doing impressions of the Beasts, when they were surprised by the pipe-organ doorbell ringing. Ivy ran to get it, and Olivia and Sophia followed.

"Oh, hi, Georgia," Olivia heard Ivy say as she pulled open the front door.

"Goooood afternoon, Madame Ivy," a voice purred.

"Holy water!" Sophia whispered to Olivia. "It's Georgia Huntingdon, the editor of *Vamp*!"

Olivia took a step to the side so she could get a better look, but all she could make out over Ivy's shoulder was a puff of white hair.

"My dad isn't here," Ivy was saying.

"She's planning a story about a crypt that Ivy's father's working on," Sophia whispered.

"That's so cool!" Olivia squealed.

"Cool?" the voice inquired. "Did someone say 'coooool'?"

Ivy stepped aside, and Olivia finally got a good look at Georgia Huntingdon. *Wow!* she thought. The woman wore a luxurious emerald-green full-length silk coat, with jeweled buttons. She was also wearing bright red lipstick that punctuated her pale face like a smear of blood. Her hair was stark white, a beehive of curls piled atop her head and held in place with an emerald bat hairpin. Olivia couldn't tell whether she was thirty or three hundred, but she was the most stylish person she had ever seen.

"Cooool," Georgia Huntingdon purred, smiling at Olivia and revealing perfect teeth, "is about to be the new *hot*."

"But like I said," Ivy told her apologetically, closing the door to the cold, "my father's not home right now."

"Oh, I'm not here for Charles," replied Georgia. "I'm here for you. And your sister. I'm putting you two on the cover of *Vamp*."

Sophia gave an involuntary scream of excitement. Ivy seemed too stunned to speak. Georgia Huntingdon brushed past her and walked up to Olivia. She extended a cool, firm hand. "Georgia Huntingdon, *Vamp* magazine."

"Nice to meet you," Olivia replied, shaking hands.

"Does the look on your face tell me you are unfamiliar with *Vamp*?" Georgia asked.

Olivia nodded.

"We are a high-fashion monthly, catering to vaaaaaa—"

Vampires! Olivia thought.

"—rious Goth tastemakers," Georgia finished, smiling coyly. She studied Olivia's face carefully, as if trying to detect whether Olivia had noticed her slipup.

Olivia decided to play dumb, since no one was supposed to know she was in on the vampire secret. "Sorry, I don't read your magazine," she said, wrinkling her nose. "I'm not really into heavy metal."

Georgia laughed uproariously. "Chaaarming," she cooed. Olivia exchanged a secret look with Ivy, who nodded approvingly. It seemed Georgia had bought her innocent act.

"I'm sure your father wouldn't mind me doing a shoot right here right now?" Georgia half asked, half told Ivy as she looked around the hallway. "It wouldn't be the first time we've photographed in this house."

Ivy shrugged speechlessly.

"Excellent!" exclaimed Georgia. "Shall we

begin?" She pulled open the front door. "Kitty! Kong!" she called.

A pale woman in a dark business suit and angular glasses appeared at the front door with a clipboard. She entered and surveyed the room, silently greeting everyone with a professional smile.

That must be Kitty, thought Olivia. Behind Kitty, a bald man with huge muscles and a tight black top appeared with an armful of camera equipment. *And that must be Kong!*

Georgia beckoned to the girls as Kitty and Kong began scurrying around. "I am sorry for the short notice, but we are on a verrrrry tight deadline," she said. "The magazine comes out on Wednesday, and I only just learned of your story—but it's much too big to leave for the next issue. Don't you agree?" Suddenly her eyes fell on Sophia.

"Who are you? A trrrriplet?" she said, rolling her "r" mercilessly. Then she gave a full-throated laugh.

"My name's Sophia Hewitt," Sophia said, shaking Georgia's hand firmly. "As an aspiring photographer myself, I am a huge fan of your magazine, Ms. Huntingdon."

"Oh?" Georgia said. "Then how would you like to assist Kong today?"

Sophia tried to speak, but all she could do was wiggle around excitedly. It was like she'd been turned into a jellyfish.

"Go on," Georgia smiled, waving her away to where the muscle-bound photographer was unpacking some lights across the room.

As Sophia went to help Kong, Kitty appeared, pushing an enormous rack of clothes with each hand—one filled with dresses in shimmering dark shades, the other with lighter and brighter ones. On the second rack, Olivia immediately noticed an ivory satin sleeveless cowl-necked gown that looked like something Marilyn Monroe would have worn. She reached to look at the label. "Is this a real Margot Chenille?" she gasped.

"Of course!" exclaimed Georgia.

Ivy fingered a sequined black flapper dress with a fringed bottom. "How do we know what will fit?"

"It all will," Georgia answered with an obvious gesture, "because Kitty has only selected the latest fashions in your size."

Olivia and Ivy exchanged excited looks—Olivia could tell her sister was nervous about all the attention, as usual, but they were both total fashion hounds.

For the first shot, Kitty had draped a pale sash of silk dramatically over a chaise longue in the foyer. After consulting with Kong, Sophia helped pick the sisters' outfits. For Olivia, they chose a bright pink Coco Loco cocktail dress with a form-fitting sleeveless top, while Ivy wore a midnight-blue off-the-shoulder number from Before Dawn.

This is so fun! Olivia thought, carefully walking to the chaise in her specially selected, superhigh heels.

"Olivia," Kong's deep voice boomed from behind his camera, "I want you to make a face like you are blowing the biggest bubble gum bubble ever." Olivia puffed up her cheeks and widened her eyes. "Bigger!" Kong commanded. "Bigger!" Olivia felt like her face was going to pop off.

"Now, Ivy, pretend to pop your sister's bubble," Kong instructed.

"Yessss!" Olivia heard Georgia hiss approvingly as Kong's flash started popping.

After a few minutes, Georgia clapped her hands briskly. "The camera looooves you," she said. "Time for the next outfit!" and whisked them away to change.

Next, Olivia and Ivy put on matching tight satin dresses, except Olivia's was white while Ivy's was black. The dresses had this really cool thing happening, like they were being peeled back layer by layer as they rose up the body, from tons of fabric on the bottom to just a thin layer on top. Ivy looked gorgeous. *I guess since we're identical twins,* Olivia realized happily, *that means I look gorgeous, too!*

Georgia led them to an alcove off the front hall, where there was a grand piano. "Could there be a more perfect backdrop?" she enthused. "The caption will read: 'Ivy and Olivia, ebony and ivory, make music together!'" Sophia directed Ivy to sit at the keyboard, while Kong had Olivia take off her shoes and sit on top of the piano.

Kong told Olivia to pose like a lounge singer, while Ivy pretended to play the piano. They finished with both girls standing atop the piano, holding their high-heeled shoes in their hands and shouting the words to "I Wear My Sunglasses at Night." Georgia and her crew looked ecstatic.

Then Olivia changed into a luxurious burgundy satin ball gown, while Ivy slipped into a dark green one that trailed onto the stone floor, and they posed next to one of the balusters at the bottom of the main staircase. Olivia felt just like a character in the Count Vira novels she loved so much.

Kong handed the camera to Sophia to let her take some pictures.

"More drama! More passion!" Sophia called enthusiastically.

Ivy stood beside Olivia on the bottom stair, one hand on the balustrade and the other on her hip, while Olivia tried to accentuate her cheekbones for the camera.

After Sophia gave the camera back, Olivia saw her whispering in Kong's ear. Then Kong waved Georgia over and Sophia continued whispering to the two of them. Kong's bald head bobbed enthusiastically on his enormous shoulders.

"Young lady," Olivia heard Georgia say at last,

"when you are of working age, you will call me."
Then she turned away. "Kitty!" she called, "I
want every drop of makeup off these girls."

Once their faces were completely clean, Kitty
told Olivia and Ivy to follow her to the guest bathroom on the second floor. Olivia thought it was so
they could change again, but when she got there,
Kong and Sophia were setting up lights.

Sophia came over. "This is going to be killer,"
she said. She gestured to a tall, ornate oval mirror
that leaned up against one wall. "We're going to
shoot you so you're looking at yourselves in the
mirror. Except you won't be able to see the camera in the shot."

"You can do that?" Ivy wondered.

"I read about it in a book," Sophia said under
her breath. "We have to get the angle exactly right."

A few minutes later, Olivia and Ivy were posing
next to each other, Olivia in a simple white shift
dress and Ivy in a simple black one. Olivia stared
at the reflection of herself and her sister. Their skin
tones were different, of course, and their eye color,
but otherwise they looked, well . . . *identical*.

"Olivia?" Ivy murmured.

"Yeah?" said Olivia, trying not to break the pose which Kong had just carefully orchestrated.

"I think I see my reflection," Ivy whispered, "and it's you!"

CHAPTER 7

A little girl with long black hair and black whiskers drawn on her face opened the door to Brendan's house and shrieked at the top of her lungs, "IVY'S SISTER'S HERE!!!" Then she grabbed Olivia's hand and pulled her inside. "Want to see my room?"

"Um," Olivia said, glancing around. "Is Brendan home?"

"His room's boring." The little girl sighed, rolling her eyes. "Come on!" she said, dragging Olivia toward the stairs.

"What's your name?" Olivia asked.

"I'm Bethany," the little girl declared. "And

I'm seven, but I'm utterly mature."

Bethany pushed open a door that had a DO NOT EXPOSE TO SUNLIGHT sign on it.

"So you're a cheerleader?" Bethany asked. Olivia nodded. "I think cheerleaders suck. Look!" she said, kneeling down in front of a black dollhouse. She reached into a tiny bathroom and produced a Barbie doll that had red pom-poms glued to her hands. "Do you like her? She lives in the bathtub."

Olivia laughed, taking off her jacket. "Does she know any cheers?"

Bethany nodded and made the doll hop around on the floor. "Two, four, six, eight. The bunny hop is really great!"

Olivia made the sound of a roaring crowd.

Bethany giggled. Then she said, "Will you come play with me after Ivy moves away?"

Olivia felt an ache deep in her heart. She nodded silently.

Bethany smiled gratefully, even though her eyes were on her doll, which she was making do somersaults. "I'm going to miss Ivy," she said quietly.

"Me, too," whispered Olivia.

"Here you are," a familiar voice announced. Olivia looked up to see Ivy standing in the doorway. "Everyone's waiting to meet you in the kitchen," Ivy told her. "Hey, Bethany," she said, "want to do the spider?"

"Yeah!" Bethany shrieked. She ran up to Ivy, then turned around, put her hands on the ground, and flipped her legs up into the air. Ivy caught them and steered the little girl down the stairs like a wheelbarrow as Olivia followed.

"Did Olivia tell you that we're going to be in *Vamp*?" Ivy said to the soles of Bethany's feet.

"You are not!" Bethany lifted one hand off the ground and twisted around to look up at them.

"We are," Olivia confirmed. "Maybe we'll autograph a copy for you."

Bethany squealed and spun back around.

When they entered the kitchen, a middle-aged man with crazy gray hair and round glasses hurried across the room. "You must be Olivia," he said excitedly. His gaze flicked from Olivia to Ivy. For a moment, Mr. Daniels seemed completely lost in his own thoughts. Brendan came up and gave Olivia a hug.

Brendan's father leaned forward and peered into Olivia's ear. "Inconceivable!" he murmured.

"Dad?" Brendan said in an embarrassed voice, and Mr. Daniels snapped out of it.

"Oh, yes!" Brendan's father blurted. "I mean, yes, inconceivable how much you and Ivy look alike." He took off his glasses and polished them with his shirt. "Not that it's amazing for twins to look alike. Just that you're so different." He laughed uncomfortably. "But not *too* different. Oh, dear," he finished, suddenly shutting himself up and putting his glasses back on.

Olivia could tell Mr. Daniels was trying desperately not to give anything vampish away, but she just nodded like she had no idea what he was fussing about.

A woman wearing a gray pin-striped blouse tucked into black slacks gave Olivia a warm smile. "What my husband is trying to say is that it's a pleasure to meet you," she said, coming over to give Olivia a peck on the cheek. "I'm Brendan's mom." She handed her husband some long tongs. "We're cooking on the barbecue grill outside," she explained. "But, don't worry, we're eating indoors."

A few minutes later, Mr. Daniels, now wearing an apron and clutching the barbecue tongs, stopped next to where Olivia and Ivy were sitting at the kitchen table. "So, Olivia," he said, clearly trying to sound casual, "what are your favorite foods?"

"Tofu," she answered.

"Ew!" cried Bethany from where she and Brendan were playing with toy elephants on the floor.

"Inconceivable," Mr. Daniels muttered again. His eyes focused on her shoulder. "Hmmm," he said, unconsciously reaching down and plucking a loose strand of hair from Olivia's shirt.

Just then, Mrs. Daniels came over with some pink lemonade. While Olivia was taking the glass, she saw Mr. Daniels carefully put the hair into his shirt pocket.

I bet he's going to test my DNA, Olivia thought, slightly weirded out. *But I guess one hair won't hurt.*

Mr. Daniels ventured outside to cook, leaving the door open so he could still join in the conversation.

"So tell me," Mrs. Daniels said to Ivy and Olivia, "what was it like when you two first met?"

"Surreal," Olivia and Ivy both said at once.

Mrs. Daniels nodded like she understood. She exchanged glances with her husband. "You must have wanted to share all your secrets with each other right away."

Ivy shot Olivia a paranoid look, clearly worried that the Daniels were onto them. Olivia studied Brendan's parents' faces: Mrs. Daniels looked so sympathetic, and Mr. Daniels seemed so eager. *They want to talk openly,* Olivia thought, *just as badly as we do.* She looked at Ivy hopefully, but her sister responded with a brisk shake of her head.

Bethany suddenly came over to the sisters, twirling like a top. "I can't *believe* you're going to be in *Vamp* magazine," she shrieked, "with all the most famous vampires in the world!"

Mrs. Daniels breathed in sharply, and outside, Mr. Daniels's barbecue tongs clattered to the patio. Ivy looked completely panicked and Bethany suddenly froze, mid-swoon, realizing what she'd done.

"Oops," she squeaked.

"You didn't really mean vampires," Mrs. Daniels said hurriedly, "did you, dear? That was just your little game."

"Q-quite an imagination," Mr. Daniels stammered, coming inside.

All at once, tears began pouring out of Bethany's eyes, making her whiskers run. "Am I going to be condemned?" she bawled.

Mrs. Daniels bent down to comfort her as everyone averted their eyes. Olivia felt *terrible*. Bethany was clearly going to be scarred for life if Olivia didn't let her off the hook. She crept up and took the little girl's hand.

"There aren't any vampires, I swear!" Bethany sobbed, shaking her head wildly at Olivia, her face soaked with tears.

"Bethany, it's okay," Olivia responded kindly. "I already knew."

★ 🦇 ★

We're staked! Ivy thought, her stomach sinking as she waited for horror to spread across the faces of Brendan's parents. Instead, Mr. and Mrs. Daniels exchanged knowing looks, and Mr. Daniels bent down before his daughter.

"My nightingale," he said, "you must never, never talk about vampires." He glanced toward Olivia. "Especially when there is anyone around that you're not absolutely sure is one of us. Do you understand?"

Bethany nodded and wiped her nose on her sleeve.

Mr. and Mrs. Daniels turned to Ivy.

Brendan's parents are going to hate me forever! she thought. "I didn't mean to break the First Law," she blurted.

"Of course you didn't," Mrs. Daniels said. "But how could you not have? Olivia's your twin sister, after all."

Brendan came up behind Ivy and gave her shoulder a supportive squeeze.

"This is an exceptional case," Mr. Daniels agreed.

Ivy felt relief spreading over her. It was like walking out of hot sun into cool shade.

"Remember the last time a human was told, Marc?" said Mrs. Daniels.

"I thought I was like the only one ever,"

Olivia said nervously.

"It is very rare," Mr. Daniels admitted, "but a handful of humans have learned the Blood Secret."

"Of course, there was a time when anyone who discovered the existence of vampires was killed," Mrs. Daniels said. Ivy noticed her sister turn white. "But things are different now."

"What happened the last time?" Ivy inquired.

"His name was Karl Lazar," Mr. Daniels said, stroking his chin. "The story made quite a scandal in the black papers, because he was the son of a vampire count. And Karl didn't just break the First Law. He broke the Second Law, too."

"Falling in love with a human," Mrs. Daniels clarified. *That's what must have happened with our parents*, Ivy thought.

"Yuck!" little Bethany exclaimed.

"So what happened to him?" Ivy asked uneasily.

"The Lazar clan was strongly separationist," Mr. Daniels said. "It was the worst of all possible situations." Ivy thought of her father, and how he refused to meet Olivia.

"Karl ended up in exile, living with his human mate. He was completely isolated from his community and his family," Mrs. Daniels concluded, and Ivy felt like a tiny stone had dropped inside her stomach and hit the dark bottom. *Is that how I'm going to end up, cast out because of my relationship with my sister?* she thought.

Mrs. Daniels looked at her children tenderly. "I don't know how parents could stand to sever themselves from their own children in that way."

A few minutes later Mr. Daniels unobtrusively gestured to Ivy that he wanted her to come outside to the barbecue. Ivy hurried over. Mr. Daniels was turning steaks. He pointed with his tongs at an unappetizing brown disk in one corner. "Do you have any idea how to cook one of these veggie burgers?" he asked in a low voice.

Ivy shrugged apologetically.

"The things humans find appetizing," Mr. Daniels murmured. "Inconceivable!" The smoke rising around his head made his wild mane of gray hair appear even larger.

"Olivia and I read your research online," Ivy said. "Do you really think it's impossible for a vamp and a human to have babies?"

Mr. Daniels's glasses flickered with the reflection of the barbecue's flames. "That is *exactly* why I find you and Olivia so extraordinary," he said. "Science is the study of empirical evidence. It is about what we can prove physically. And the existence of twin sisters, one vampire and one human, is nothing if not physical proof. I'm not certain *what* the two of you prove exactly. But we shall find out!"

He grabbed a fork from beside the barbecue and speared the veggie burger. "Imagine this is human DNA, the fundamental building block of human life," he said. In his other hand, he picked up a huge steak with his tongs. "While this is vampire DNA, the essence of our existence. My research says they are incompatible." He flung them both back on the barbecue, and the flames flared wildly. "But perhaps there is something we are missing."

He sighed thoughtfully. "Perhaps," he continued, "the helical structure of human DNA can be made to intermingle with the helical structure of *our* DNA." He began spouting hypotheses. Ivy had no clue what he was talking about, but the cloud of smoke around his head was getting larger.

"Marc," Mrs. Daniels called from the kitchen, "is something burning?"

Ivy and Mr. Daniels looked down at the barbecue. He quickly flipped everything over.

"I'd like you and Olivia to come down to V-Gen," he said. "My colleagues would be very excited to meet you. Of course," he went on in a low voice, "you should probably pretend Olivia doesn't know about vampires. Who knows how ASHH might feel about that."

"What's ASHH?" Ivy asked, waving Olivia over from where she and Brendan were playing death tag with Bethany.

"The Agency for the Security of Human Hybrids," Mr. Daniels explained.

"That sounds ominous," Ivy remarked.

"There have always been legends in the vampire community about the horrific results that ensue when a human and a vampire mate," Brendan's father said.

"Like how I used to have four heads?" Olivia interrupted.

Brendan's dad did a double take.

"She's joking," Ivy clarified.

"Of course," Mr. Daniels said sheepishly. "In any case, it's been a source of great paranoia. Vampires are terribly worried that a human and a vampire will produce some sort of monster, which might cause our existence to be revealed. For this reason, ASHH was set up by the Vampire Round Table to investigate reports of vampire-human relationships. It's all nonsense, of course," he said, "but ASHH checks into each and every tabloid headline about a deformed offspring. They're kept quite busy, as you might imagine."

"Have they ever discovered any actual hybrids?" asked Ivy. *Maybe that's what Olivia and I are,* she thought with a shiver.

"Not a single one," Mr. Daniels answered. "I personally believe ASHH isn't worth what it costs to run, but unfortunately I'm in the minority. And in any case they do do *some* good work—including funding a few projects for V-Gen." He leaned close to the girls. "It helps that the agency's office is in our building, but they do tend to poke their noses into our business more than I'd like."

"Do you think they have files about us?" Ivy asked apprehensively. Olivia nodded like she'd been about to ask the same question.

"If they don't already," Brendan's father said, "I expect they soon will. But don't worry," he added upon seeing Ivy and Olivia's reaction. "Since you two being twins has become so public, ASHH wouldn't dare kidnap you for study."

Somehow, thought Ivy, *that doesn't make me feel better.*

"Um, Mr. Daniels?" Olivia said, gesturing to the barbecue.

Mr. Daniels quickly picked up Olivia's veggie burger—now charred and smoking—and dangled it in the air with his tongs. "Do you think this is done?"

★ 🐰 ★

Olivia's mom was planning to pick Olivia up from Ivy's house later, so the sisters decided to walk there from Brendan's. Most of the way, Olivia and Ivy didn't say much. Olivia was lost in her thoughts about what it would be like to have vampire parents. The Daniels were the first vamp grown-ups she'd spent time with. In some ways, they were just like normal parents. In others, they seemed much more . . . knowing.

As they climbed the long driveway, lined with bare trees, Ivy clicked her tongue thoughtfully.

"What are you thinking about?" asked Olivia.

"ASHH," Ivy answered. "About how maybe *they're* the reason there's no record of my adoption. They could have covered it up."

"Why would they?"

"Maybe they were trying to bury my connection to a human sister," Ivy said, unlocking the front door. "For all we know, they orchestrated our split from the very beginning."

The thought sent a chill through Olivia. Her eyes took a moment to adjust to the dim lighting in Ivy's front hall, but her sister was already heading for the living room. Olivia hurried to catch up.

As they passed through the living room archway, Ivy stopped in her tracks, and Olivia walked right into her back. Over her sister's shoulder, Olivia could see the back of a black-suited specter standing in the middle of the living room.

It's ASHH! Olivia thought.

The man turned and looked at the girls sternly.

"Hi, Dad," said Ivy.

★ 🦇 ★

Ivy's father just stood there. He didn't even say hi. Finally, Ivy said, "Olivia, this is my father."

Olivia bounced over. "It's so great to finally meet you!" she said, but Ivy could see that her father's jaw was clenched. He forced himself to smile and, avoiding Olivia's eyes, shook her hand once before withdrawing. It was like he didn't even want to touch her.

Ivy's blood started to simmer. *I can't believe he's being so prejudiced!* she thought.

They all stared at one another until finally Ivy couldn't take it anymore. "Is it okay if Olivia and I use the computer?" she asked.

"No," her father dismissed. "I need it for work."

"It won't be for long," Ivy argued. "Olivia has to go home soon anyway."

"I have a great deal of preparing to do before we move, Ivy," he said abruptly.

Ivy's vision suddenly blurred. "I don't care about the move!" she shouted. "I care about Olivia. I care about my sister—unlike *you*!"

Her father's face changed, and his eyes flickered toward Olivia for the first time. "Ivy—" he began.

"I care about my *real* parents!" Ivy screamed. Stricken, her father staggered backward, steadying himself against the edge of the couch.

"Sorry to bother you," Olivia said sadly to Mr. Vega as Ivy grabbed her hand and stalked out.

CHAPTER 8

The next day at lunch, Ivy saw her sister approaching across the cafeteria and dried her eyes with her napkin. She'd just been unloading on Sophia and Brendan about her fight with her father.

"How are you?" Olivia asked gently.

Ivy shrugged. "I'd be better if my dad wasn't so narrow-minded." She moved her bag so Olivia could sit down.

"I don't understand," Sophia said. "Charles Vega has always been the vamp dad everyone wanted." Brendan nodded in agreement.

"Come on," Ivy said with an eye roll. "He

never liked humans."

"Remember when he decorated that human lady's house in LA?" Sophia said. "That didn't seem to put his wings in a flap."

"That was just a client," Ivy said, shaking her head. "Anyway," she said, deciding to change the subject, "I looked on the VVV last night to see if I could access ASHH files."

Olivia perked up. "And?"

"I couldn't," Ivy revealed. "If we want to find out anything, we're going to have to go to the ASHH office ourselves."

"Do you think we can ask for our files just like that?" Olivia wondered.

"I wasn't thinking of asking," Ivy replied with a mischievous smile. "I was thinking of sneaking in and digging around."

Brendan spit a gulp of cranberry juice back into his cup.

"Bad Ivy," Sophia said, shaking her finger teasingly. "Bad, bad Ivy!"

Olivia leaned forward. "Could we actually do that?" she asked in a low voice.

"Brendan's dad invited us to the V-Gen

offices," Ivy said, "and they're in the same building. So we already have an excuse to get in and out of the compound. All we need is a distraction," she said, putting her arm around Brendan and squeezing his shoulder, "so we can get in and out of the ASHH offices without anyone noticing."

Brendan frowned. "Is 'distraction' a code word for 'boyfriend'?"

Ivy grinned. "Maybe."

"This'll be interesting," Brendan assented with a playful roll of his eyes.

"How about this afternoon after school?" Ivy proposed with a conspiratorial glance toward Olivia.

"There's no better time than the present," Olivia agreed, and Brendan nodded.

"What about me?" Sophia interjected. "What can I do?"

"Somebody has to stay behind to tell our story," Ivy told her, "in case we end up being abducted."

"You're joking, right?" said Sophia.

A chill flashed over Ivy. "I hope so," she said.

★ 🐰 ★

After school, Olivia, Ivy, and Brendan caught a bus to Brendan's father's office complex across town. Brendan had called his dad to let him know they were coming, while Olivia had called her mom and explained that she was doing a research project with Ivy—which was totally true. As for Ivy, she wasn't talking to her father, so she didn't tell him anything.

Eventually, the three of them were the only passengers left on the bus, and all Olivia could see from the window was one gray office building after another, against the wintry gray sky. Arriving at the end of a cul-de-sac, the driver called, "Last stop, Pentagram Court."

Jumping down off the bus, Olivia found herself staring up at a hulking black glass building, glistening in the afternoon sun like a dark jewel. It was surrounded by a security gate, and the bus had let them off right in front of a guardhouse.

"Can I help you?" a pale security officer inquired.

"We're here to see Marc Daniels at V-Gen," Brendan announced.

Olivia glanced up and spotted a security

camera sitting atop the gate, aimed right at her. She shifted uncomfortably as the camera looked her up and down with a whir, from her pink corduroy jacket down to her cheerleading sneakers. "No civilians allowed," the guard said stonily.

"He's expecting *all* of us," Brendan replied firmly.

The security guard looked unconvinced. "Names?"

"Brendan, Ivy, and Olivia," Brendan answered.

The guard disappeared into his booth. Olivia could see him through the window talking on the phone. After he hung up, he slid the glass open and handed down three guest passes. As they put them around their necks, the gate clanked and slid open.

Inside the enormous black marble lobby, Mr. Daniels was waiting in his white lab coat. "Ivy, Olivia!" he said warmly, shaking their hands and giving Brendan a quick hug. "I'm so glad you came so soon!"

As they all waited for the elevator, Ivy nudged Olivia's arm and silently nodded toward the building directory that was hanging on the wall.

Olivia's eyes immediately zeroed in on what her sister was looking at:

ASHH   2A

V-GEN   2C

Brendan's dad's lab and ASHH are on the same floor! thought Olivia. *Perfect!*

When the elevator doors opened onto the second floor, Ivy, Olivia, and Brendan followed Mr. Daniels to the left, but Olivia used the opportunity to steal a backward glance. There, at the opposite end of the hall past a tall potted plant was a dark wall with ASHH on it in enormous, luminous letters. Beside the letters was a door, and beside the door stood the tallest security guard Olivia had ever seen, fiddling distractedly with a walkie-talkie.

Mr. Daniels continued to the end of the hall, where a glistening sign read V-GEN PHARMACEUTI-CALS. He turned left and stopped outside a stainless steel door.

He opened the door and led the way into a

huge laboratory, filled with blinking consoles and mysterious equipment. A group of people in white lab coats were hunched around a table, arguing in low voices over some papers.

"But how could she have survived the hemoglobic transition?" Olivia heard one say.

Mr. Daniels cleared his throat loudly, and the conversation stopped abruptly. One of the group, a woman with her hair in a bun, tried to subtly turn over the sheets of paper on the table.

"Lab technicians, this is Ivy Vega," Mr. Daniels announced as they all got to their feet. "And this is her identical twin sister, Olivia Abbott."

For a moment, the scientists just stared at them. Then one started clapping, and they all erupted into applause.

Olivia grinned while Ivy shifted in her boots, uncomfortable with the attention as usual.

"What am I, garlic hummus?" Brendan whispered sarcastically as the applause died down.

"The occurrence of identical twins is a unique genetic phenomenon, and there is much we stand to learn from it," Mr. Daniels said. "These young ladies have generously agreed to allow themselves to be subject to our experimentation."

Experimentation? Olivia thought uneasily.

The lab technicians all whispered to one another excitedly.

"Ms. Voxen, will you please prepare the VMG?" Mr. Daniels asked, and the woman with the bun gave a businesslike nod before disappearing. "Everyone else to your workstations." The technicians scurried off in all directions.

Mr. Daniels led the girls past a bank of flickering screens, where two of the technicians sat in swivel chairs, frantically turning dials. As Olivia walked past, the technicians abruptly stood up to face her. "Welcome, welcome," they said nervously, weaving back and forth.

They're trying to hide the screens! thought Olivia.

Mr. Daniels stopped in the corner, where a thick, blocky wooden chair stood on a small pedestal. Across from it, Ms. Voxen stood behind a console. Wires extended from the chair in all directions, and a metal circle hung above it, waiting to be lowered onto someone's head.

"Olivia, you can sit there," Mr. Daniels said nonchalantly, gesturing with his pen.

"You mean the electric chair?" Olivia croaked.

"The what?" Mr. Daniels said. Then he laughed. "Oh, no, that's just the VMG."

Olivia looked at Ivy and Brendan desperately, but they just shrugged.

She tried to put on a brave face as she sat down. Ms. Voxen came and fastened electrodes to Olivia's temples, her neck, and each of her fingers, then secured the metal band around Olivia's head.

"This isn't going to hurt, right?" Olivia quavered.

"Just relax," responded Ms. Voxen.

You didn't answer the question, Olivia thought nervously as she watched Ms. Voxen return to her console and put on chunky sunglasses. Suddenly, Mr. Daniels and Brendan and Ivy were wearing sunglasses, too. They looked like some sort of deranged rap group.

"Commence VMG?" Ms. Voxen asked.

"Commence," Mr. Daniels answered, and Olivia thought she was going to hyperventilate as Ms. Voxen reached behind her and pulled a huge red lever.

As far as Olivia could tell, nothing happened. But Mr. Daniels and Ms. Voxen started to lean over the console, whispering excitedly and pointing at the screen.

"Is this thing even on?" Olivia asked.

Mr. Daniels looked up briefly. "That's a very interesting question, Olivia."

Olivia thought that was a strange response until it was Ivy's turn. The moment they turned the machine on with Ivy in the hot seat, Ivy's eyelids closed and started fluttering.

"Is she okay?" Olivia asked anxiously from the side.

"Of course. She's simply dreaming," Mr. Daniels explained.

Ivy and I really are *different,* thought Olivia, impressed that a machine which had no effect on her could immediately put her sister to sleep.

When they were done with the VMG, Mr. Daniels led them through the laboratory on their way to another test. Near the center of the lab, Olivia passed a tall glass box displayed proudly on a pedestal. Squinting, Olivia could just make out two vertical hairs, stretched taut across a metal frame. The strands were labeled OLIVIA and IVY. *It's the hair Mr. Daniels collected at his house!* she thought. *How cool is that?*

Over the next hour, she and her sister underwent one test after another. Neither of them had ever had an MRI before—they had to change into drafty gray gowns and lie totally still inside a huge aluminium tube that made ominous clanking noises. Olivia could just hear Camilla's voice in her head, saying, "It's the year 2030 and you are suspended in a cryogenic pod for your journey."

They were given X-rays, too. Then there were exercise tests, which were so *not* fair. Olivia must have sprinted like two miles on her treadmill before she collapsed. Ivy hadn't even broken a sweat.

Finally, Mr. Daniels led the girls back to where Brendan was sitting, waiting with their bags underneath a faded public health sign.

"I can't thank the two of you enough," Mr. Daniels said to Olivia and Ivy. "The results of today's experiments could change the way we think about identical twins." He winked at the girls. Around the lab, technicians were buzzing excitedly, comparing notes.

"Can you tell us the results?" Olivia asked eagerly.

Mr. Daniels shrugged. "It could take months, or even years, before we complete our analyses. In genetics, there are often more questions than answers. We'd like to have you back for more tests in one year."

A year? Olivia thought incredulously. *Ivy's leaving in like three weeks!*

She could tell Ivy was disappointed, too. Brendan just gave a little cough.

"Allow me to show you out," Mr. Daniels said.

As Brendan stood up with their bags, he started to hack.

"Are you all right, Brendan?" his father asked.

Brendan nodded. "Just a little nauseous and dizzy," he croaked. Then he staggered, and Olivia saw that his cheeks were pink.

Vampires only redden when they're about to faint! she remembered.

The girls' bags fell to the ground. Mr. Daniels lunged for his son as Brendan's legs folded.

"Ms. Voxen! Mr. Azure!" he called, struggling to hold Brendan up. The technicians rushed over.

Seeing Brendan, their eyes filled with fear.

"He must have been exposed to the V-rus!" Mr. Azure cried.

"He's displaying all the symptoms," Ms. Voxen agreed, her voice filled with panic.

"What's the V-rus?" Olivia asked.

"It doesn't concern your kind!" Mr. Azure cried, but Ms. Voxen poked him in the ribs. "I m-mean," he stuttered, "those who never had . . . er . . . chicken pox as children."

"Brendan, can you hear me?" his father asked desperately.

"Father," Brendan replied in a dreamy voice. "Is that you?"

"Mr. Spackle," Mr. Daniels called urgently to another technician, "get the V-rus treatment kit at once!"

★ 🦇 ★

As Brendan lay sprawled on the laboratory floor, Ivy stood staring at the sign that hung above where he'd been sitting: V-RUS PREVENTION AND DETECTION. SYMPTOMS: COUGHING, DIZZINESS, PINKNESS, FAINTNESS, AND NAUSEA, it read in huge faded red letters.

She looked back down at Brendan, who was now surrounded by lab technicians. Between their legs she caught his eye—and he winked!

"Ooooohhhh," Brendan moaned, shutting his eyes again. Next to his foot, the corner of a pink compact peeked out of Olivia's open bag where he'd dropped it. *He used blush to make himself look pink!* Ivy thought.

She grabbed Olivia's hand. "Let's go," she whispered, heading for the door.

"We can't—" Olivia began, but Ivy threw her a meaningful look and then she caught on. "Oh, right . . ." she murmured, falling in behind her sister.

Olivia shut the door behind them and the commotion of Brendan's "emergency" disappeared. Ivy crept up and peeked around the hallway corner.

At the other end, the lone, giant security guard stood with his arms crossed impassively beside the entrance to ASHH. The office's doors slid open with a mechanical hiss, and Ivy quickly drew back. Slowly, carefully, she peeked out again.

A short bald guy in a black tie and trench coat had come out of ASHH. "Have a good night, Frankie," the man said in a nasal voice. "Everything's turned off. I'm the last one."

Ivy heard the security guard grunt in acknowledgment as the man made for the elevators.

Ivy turned to Olivia. "The office is empty," she whispered. "I don't see a keypad or card slot or anything. We just have to get past the security guard."

"Who's only, like, the size of the Washington Monument!" replied Olivia.

"And we have to hurry," Ivy added, knowing that Brendan couldn't keep up his act forever. She stuck her head around the corner again to survey the situation.

About a third of the way down, opposite the elevators, was a fire exit with a sign that said: OPEN ONLY IN EMERGENCY. MANAGEMENT WILL BE NOTIFIED. And on the floor next to the elevators was an enormous potted plant.

"I have an idea," Ivy whispered. "Stay here."

She crawled along the carpet as fast as her vampiric speed would allow, her shoulder tight to the wall. She stopped behind the plant. Her knees ached momentarily from rug burn, but then they instantly healed. Through the plant's leaves, Ivy kept an eye on the guard, who had started pacing back and forth.

Ivy set her feet and took a deep breath. When the guard's back was turned, she pushed off into a front handspring, tapping open the fire exit with the soles of her boots. When the alarm began blaring from the stairwell, she was already tumbling back on the other side of the plant. *And I thought I'd never use my cheerleading skills,* she thought proudly.

The security guard came charging down the hall. He raced through the fire door to investigate and the heavy door slowly clanked shut behind him. Moments later, the door shook as the guard realized his mistake and tried to open it from the other side, but it was locked.

Olivia ran up, beaming. Together, she and Ivy dashed to the end of the hall. The ASHH doors whispered open obligingly, and they disappeared inside.

★ 🐇 ★

Olivia stood beside her sister inside the darkened office. She could make out rows of desks, each one topped by an ancient-looking computer. Hulking filing cabinets lined the walls.

Ivy fingered a stack of papers on a nearby desk. "Look how much paper there is in this place," she said in a discouraged voice. "We might as well be looking for a corpse in a graveyard."

Olivia's eyes focused on the only closed-off room she could see: a huge partitioned cube in the center of the office, its smoked glass walls glowing slightly in the darkness. *If I were an important file,* she thought, *that's where I'd be.* "Come on," she said.

Luckily, the door was open. Olivia flipped the light switch, and then had to squint because of all the reflected light bouncing around the room. Stainless steel filing cabinets lined the walls, except in the corners, where there were gleaming glass display cabinets filled with strange-looking artifacts. In the center of the room was a huge stainless steel slab of a table—without, oddly, any chairs around it.

They each took a filing cabinet and started

thumbing through folders. Olivia scanned the typed labels: Kulter . . . Kunz . . . Kuzin.

"Everything's filed by last name," she and Ivy announced at the same time.

"What name should we be looking for?" Ivy asked.

"How about Vega?" Olivia tried.

Ivy pulled open another cabinet. "Nope," she said after a moment.

Olivia glanced back down at her cabinet, and a label caught her eye, one that was flagged with a red dot: LAZAR. *That's the name the Daniels mentioned,* she remembered. Curious, she pulled out the file, which was nearly two inches thick, and opened it.

ASHH CASE ABSTRACT

CASE #: 6765475888-102923

NAME: KARL LAZAR

PROVENANCE: ELDEST SON OF COUNT AND COUNTESS LAZAR OF COVASNA PROVINCE, TRANSYLVANIA

SUMMARY: (1) SUBJECT IN VIOLATION OF 1ST AND 2ND LAWS OF THE NIGHT, WITH HUMAN SUSANNAH KENDALL OF ANDOVER,

MASSACHUSETTS.

(2) COUNT AND COUNTESS LAZAR IN STRICT OPPOSITION TO RELATIONSHIP.

(3) SUBJECT'S WHEREABOUTS UNKNOWN

STATUS: *POTENTIAL HYBRID ALERT!*

Olivia turned the page, and her gaze fell on a creased black-and-white photograph of a stern-looking vampire couple with their three children: a little girl and two young boys. Behind them, an imposing castle loomed ominously. *The Lazar Clan, Covasna* read the ornate caption. *Count Rolen and Countess Rochette with children Kat, Karl, and Karina.*

Olivia peered at the photo more closely. Her gaze fell on a jeweled medallion hanging around the countess's neck. There was a symbol carved in it—and it looked like an eye with a *V* inside it.

Olivia gasped. Carefully laying the file on the stainless steel table for her sister to see, she pointed with a shaking finger at the countess's necklace.

130

"It's the same symbol that's on our emeralds!" Ivy whispered.

They looked at each other in shock, and Olivia gripped her sister's hand. "I think our parents' names," Olivia said slowly, "are Karl Lazar and Susannah Kendall."

Ivy's eyes flashed. "Are you sure?" She started flipping through the file frantically as Olivia looked over her shoulder. Suddenly her black fingernail plunked down in the middle of a page. "Fourteen years ago!" Ivy said. "They disappeared *fourteen* years ago!"

"Are there any pictures of them?" Olivia asked, her heart pounding.

Ivy summarily dumped the file on the table, and they both started sifting through the papers.

"Anything about them having kids?" Ivy asked.

"No." Olivia shook her head. "Just a potential hybrid alert."

Then Olivia's hands fell on a Xeroxed newspaper clipping from *The Andover Rover*. The headline read, LOCAL, SUSANNAH KENDALL, 34, DIES IN TRAGIC ACCIDENT. Her breath caught, and she pushed the clipping in front of her sister.

Ivy closed her eyes for a moment and let out a heavy sigh. Then her eyes flew open. "The guard!" she whispered. Sure enough, Olivia could hear faint footsteps outside in the hallway. Together, they frantically shoved the pages back into their folder and shoved the folder back into the cabinet. Olivia pushed the cabinet shut as Ivy turned out the lights.

The main door of ASHH hissed open.

* 🦇 *

"Shhh," Ivy whispered to her sister. Olivia backed into a corner as the tall shadow of the guard moved slowly along the glass wall. Ivy saw a display cabinet behind her sister, with a small sign atop it that said ALARMED.

"Wait!" Ivy whispered as her sister bumped into the cabinet.

The guard's shadow on the wall froze, and Ivy and Olivia both held their breaths as the glass cabinet rocked back and forth. Ivy prayed that it wouldn't tip over and shatter. Miraculously, it righted itself.

I'm sure just a bump wouldn't set off the alarm,

Ivy thought with relief.

That's when the office flooded with flashing red lights and a blaring high-pitched noise. Ivy and her sister dove underneath the stainless steel table as the guard burst through the door.

Seeing nothing out of the ordinary, he gave a confused grunt, and moved around the table to examine the display cabinet. Olivia and Ivy carefully inched to the other side of the table, then slipped out of the door under the cover of the blaring alarm.

The main door to ASHH slid open and the twins raced through it and down the hall. The elevator beeped and started to open as they flew past it. As she rounded the corner at the V-Gen end of the hall, Ivy glanced over her shoulder to see a herd of uniformed guards stampeding out of the elevator toward ASHH.

We made it! Ivy thought, and shared a giddy look with her sister as they walked through the V-Gen lab door.

"Hey!" Brendan waved from his seat in the corner, where he was sipping a large glass of water.

"Are you okay?" Ivy ran over and hugged him with mock concern.

"I'm fine," Brendan grinned. His face was damp—somehow, he'd managed to wipe off Olivia's blush. "It must have been something I ate at the school cafeteria today."

Mr. Daniels appeared behind them. "They must stop putting garlic in everything when so many young people are allergic," he said in a serious voice. He turned to Ivy. "Where did you two disappear to?"

"We were in the ladies' room," Ivy answered quickly. "I was so anxious about Brendan's condition, I suddenly had to go." She tried to look embarrassed.

"You must have been gone for fifteen minutes," Mr. Daniels observed.

"We got locked out," Olivia stammered. "We had to get a security guard to let us back in."

"Oh, no," Mr. Daniels said with genuine concern. "Well, it appears all of us have had quite an eventful afternoon."

As the three of them skipped out of the office building arm in arm a few minutes later, Ivy and her sister debriefed Brendan on their escapade.

"That's killer," Brendan remarked. "You found out almost everything you could have hoped for!"

"Thanks to you," said Ivy, squeezing his arm.

The sun was starting to set as the three of them sat huddled on the curb in front of the guard hut waiting for the bus.

"Maybe our parents wanted to keep us secret," Ivy theorized.

"From ASHH?" Brendan asked.

Ivy nodded.

"And maybe from the whole Lazar family, too," Olivia pointed out. "After all, the Lazars didn't approve."

Ivy entwined her sister's fingers in her own and looked down at the alternating pattern of pink and black fingernails it made. She lay her head on her sister's shoulder. "At least now we know their names," she said.

"Karl and Susannah." Olivia sighed.

"Karl and Susannah." Ivy repeated thoughtfully.

CHAPTER 9

All day Tuesday, Olivia still felt giddy from their success at the ASHH offices. In fact, she was still humming to herself Wednesday morning, when Ivy and Sophia appeared at her locker while she was putting her jacket away.

"Code black." They grinned before darting away. Olivia knew from secret meetings during the Serena Star affair that that meant she should meet them in the science hall bathroom immediately. She quickly slammed her locker shut and followed them down the hall.

"With smiles like those, you two are a disgrace to Goths everywhere," Olivia teased as the bathroom door swung shut behind her. "What's up?"

Ivy bent down to make sure all the stalls were empty. When she gave a thumbs-up, Sophia reached into her black cat backpack and pulled out a magazine. She held it out to Olivia with both hands.

It was the new issue of *Vamp*. And she was on the cover! The picture was of Ivy and Olivia, looking into each other's eyes in the ornate mirror in Ivy's guest bathroom. The headline read, TWINS TO DIE FOR.

"If anyone in our community didn't suspect you knew our secret before," Sophia said proudly, "they sure will now. But nothing swings public opinion like the cover of *Vamp*."

Olivia grabbed the magazine and flipped it open. She landed right in the middle of a series of glossy pictures of her and her sister, each coupled with a little paragraph of text.

"It's eight pages long," Ivy enthused, and she and Sophia gathered around Olivia so they could all look at the same time.

There was Ivy playing the piano, while Olivia sat on top of it.

"That was such a killer idea," Sophia murmured.

There was Ivy in her cocktail dress, trying to pop a huge round pink bubble gum bubble that had been photoshopped in over Olivia's mouth.

"So cool!" said Olivia.

And there they were in front of the stairs, looking totally glammed out in their burgundy and green gowns. The last spread was the grand finale: a collage of artsy black-and-white photos of the twins together in the mirror.

"'Ivy Vega and Olivia Abbott share a bond that only blood sisters can,'" Ivy read over Olivia's shoulder. "'They laugh at each other's jokes and cry at each other's hardships. Now that they have discovered each other, they are, in a word, inseparable.'"

"Awww!" Olivia gushed. She took over reading. "'These remarkable young women have something to teach us all,'" she intoned, "'about what is possible between humans and vampires. For when there is no fear, there can be love—despite all differences.'" On the verge of tears, Olivia looked up again and saw that her sister's eyes were filling up, too.

There was only one paragraph left, but Olivia couldn't go on. Sophia gently took the magazine from her hands.

"'In a matter of weeks,'" Sophia read carefully, "'Ivy will move to Europe with her father. Having only just found each other, she and her twin shall be torn asunder yet again. But now, even distance is not enough to keep them apart'"—Sophia paused dramatically—"'for they are twins for eternity.'"

Olivia and her sister gave each other a huge hug.

"I'm going to miss you so much," Olivia whispered.

"I can't wait to make my father read this." Ivy sniffled defiantly. "Georgia sent me a full set of photos, as a souvenir to hang in my new room."

"And Kong sent me a full set of photos for my portfolio," Sophia added.

"So I can keep this copy?" asked Olivia.

"No," Sophia said abruptly, taking the magazine back. She reached into her bag and pulled out a much thinner issue. "This one's for you.

Special delivery from Georgia Huntingdon."

"What's the difference?" Olivia asked.

"No references to you know what," Sophia answered. Olivia flipped it open, and saw that the only article inside was the one about her and her sister—and even there, lots of text had been deleted.

Olivia frowned. "Can't I have a regular one? I promise I won't show anyone."

Ivy shook her head. "Yours is better."

"There's a reason we call our periodicals the 'black papers,'" Sophia explained. "They're printed on special paper with special ink, so the moment they're exposed to sunlight, the pages turn completely black. And even if they never see the light of day, they blacken in a week anyway."

At least the final spread of Olivia and her sister in the mirror remained intact. They'd only changed one line so it simply said, "These remarkable young women have something to teach us all about what is possible."

I'll treasure this for as long as I live, Olivia thought happily.

The issues of *Vamp* concealed again, Olivia

followed Ivy and Sophia out of the bathroom. They were hurrying to first-period class when Olivia saw two sixth-grade girls charging toward them, arm in arm. One was dressed all in pink and the other was totally clad in black, but in every other way, their outfits were identical.

The one in pink cried out in excitement when she spotted Ivy and Olivia. "Me and my best friend, Marta, planned our outfits," she said, her braces glinting as she spoke, "so we could be twin opposites, just like you! I'm Olivia."

"And I'm Ivy!" her black-clad friend squealed.

Olivia didn't even get a chance to respond before her sister dragged her away down the hall.

"And people think *I'm* a bloodsucker," Ivy said, clearly weirded out by their cultish look-a-likes.

"Well, I think it's fun," Olivia said proudly. Sophia just shook her head in disbelief.

Suddenly Olivia heard a familiar voice calling her name. She spun around to see Camilla chasing them down the hall, waving a newspaper in the air above her blond curls.

"Have you two seen this?" Camilla cried,

thrusting the newspaper at them.

"What?" Olivia and Ivy asked at the same time.

"You made the front page of the *Gazette*!" Camilla announced. "They reprinted Toby's article from the *Scribe* word for word!"

Camilla handed them each a copy of the local newspaper—and sure enough, there were the matching pictures of Ivy and Olivia that had appeared in the school paper the previous week.

"I almost tackled my dad for it when I saw it this morning over the breakfast table," Camilla panted.

"Where'd you get the second copy?" Ivy asked.

Camilla blushed. "I begged my next door neighbor for it, in case you both needed one."

"Thanks," said Ivy, sounding genuinely touched.

"You're the best, Camilla," Olivia said with a grin, gazing down at the front page of the *Gazette*. "Who would have thought," she marveled, "that so many people would be interested in our story?"

"Not me," Ivy groaned.

Later, at lunch, Olivia and Ivy were sitting with Brendan, Sophia, and Camilla, surrounded by a mob of people holding out newspapers and begging for autographs. Ivy looked like she wanted to crawl under the table.

Suddenly Charlotte Brown pushed in front of everyone else—except she didn't want an autograph. "I don't see what all the fuss is about," she huffed. "I mean, it's just the *Gazette*. It's not like *Teen Style* or anything."

Ivy rolled her eyes, and Olivia just smiled to herself as she signed a seventh-grade jock's newspaper, thinking, *Oh yeah? You should see our glamour shots in* Vamp*!*

Then Toby Decker came up, carrying a tray with two towering ice cream sundaes that he'd made at the dessert bar. He looked *so* excited—after all, it was his story the *Gazette* had reprinted. "You two gave me the biggest scoop of my life!" he exclaimed, setting a sundae down in front of each of them. "The least I could do is give you yours!"

"Thanks, Toby," Olivia and Ivy said.

Both their mouths were full of ice cream when Sophia snapped a picture. "Who knows what publication this might end up in?" she said excitedly.

* 🦇 *

Ivy was glad to walk into the library with Olivia after school, to research their biological parents on the regular Internet. *At least in here,* she thought, *people will have to shut their boxes about us for a second.*

It was like the whole school had gone batty. It was strange enough when the *Scribe* came out, but now it seemed like everyone was idolizing them. Vera had come up to Ivy and Olivia at the beginning of science, and Ivy had expected a fight. Instead, Vera just smiled sheepishly, apologized for the way she'd been acting, and asked for their autographs like everyone else.

Fame is like blood, Ivy thought. *Everybody wants a sip.*

She and Olivia sat down next to each other at a computer in the corner of the library. Olivia started by doing a search for "Lazar," and a bunch of results came up: *A noble history of*

Covasna, Transylvanian aristocracy, the Lazar mines. Olivia clicked through a bunch of them, but mostly all she found was brief, cryptic mentions. In fact, apart from the fact that the Lazar family had made their fortune in mining, the girls didn't find out anything they didn't already know. And they didn't find any pictures.

"There's an old saying in our community," Ivy said. "'There's only one thing more secretive than a vampire: a vampire aristocrat.'"

"Apparently," said Olivia. Next, they tried searching "Susannah Kendall Owl Creek," but nothing came up.

"Didn't the ASHH file say she was from Massachusetts?" Ivy recalled.

Olivia typed "Susannah Kendall Andover," and one link appeared. Ivy held her breath as the screen filled with a black-and-white newspaper photo of a woman in a patterned, V-necked blouse framed by lustrous, shoulder-length hair, laughing warmly at something off to the side. Her eyes sparkled. At the top of the page was a newspaper headline: LOCAL, SUSANNAH KENDALL, 34, DIES IN TRAGIC ACCIDENT. It was the same as the one they'd found in the ASHH files—except at ASHH, the article had been clipped without the photograph.

"There she is," Olivia whispered.

"She has our nose," noted Ivy.

"And our eyebrows," Olivia agreed. "I'm going to pay to print out two copies, one for each of us. Okay?"

"Thanks," Ivy said simply, and then she was alone in front of the screen. *Susannah Kendall of Andover died suddenly in a tragic accident yesterday,* the article began. *She was 34.*

Ivy was still thinking about that when her sister returned. Olivia sat down and quietly read aloud from one of the printouts in her hand.

"'Susannah was a warm, fun, and generous soul, always opening her heart to others. Blessed with a sharp wit and a keen mind, she made an impression on all who met her.'"

Olivia struggled to read the last line of the article. "'Susannah will be sorely missed.'" She dragged her eyes away from the paper at last. "That's it." She shrugged. "No mention of a husband. No mention of us."

"They were in hiding," Ivy said simply. For a moment, neither she nor her sister said anything. *I never knew I lost my real mom,* Ivy was thinking. *I only knew my dad found me, and that made everything okay.*

"I feel so lucky my parents adopted me," Olivia echoed aloud.

"I guess," Ivy said slowly, "we both ended up right where we belonged."

"It's nice to know where we came from, though," admitted Olivia, a small smile breaking across her face.

Ivy nodded. "And, now that we know Susannah was our mom and Karl Lazar was our dad, we know you definitely had a vampire parent," she pointed out. "All the Veras of the world won't be able to complain about you knowing the secret."

Olivia glanced over her shoulder to make sure no one was eavesdropping. "Does that mean I have to start shopping at BloodMart?" she joked.

A few minutes later, they were just leaving school when Ivy saw her father pacing ominously at the bottom of the deserted steps. He was clearly waiting for them.

When he saw them coming, he charged up, meeting them halfway. "Is it true that the two of you broke into the offices of ASHH?" he demanded angrily.

Ivy and Olivia exchanged panicked looks, which immediately gave them away.

"How could you, Ivy?" her father said, his voice filled with disappointment.

"How could I what?" Ivy snapped. "How could I want to know about my real parents? Olivia and I have a right to know!"

"You took a human into a restricted area!" her father said. "Did it fail to occur to you that there would be security cameras capturing your every move?" His voice dropped to an urgent whisper. "The Vampire Round Table came to our house today. Olivia is being called for an initiation!"

Ivy froze. "A what?"

"A ritual," he explained, "to test whether she is worthy of the Blood Secret."

"Uh-oh," Olivia said under her breath.

"But why?" Ivy gasped.

"*Why?*" her father repeated in exasperation.

"Because, between the article in *Vamp* and the footage of Olivia at ASHH, they have deduced that there has been a violation of the First Law of the Night!"

"Is she going to be hurt?" Ivy asked.

"Hurt?" cried Olivia.

"I don't know exactly," Ivy's father answered with a shake of his head, his anger suddenly faltering.

"But what does she have to do?" Ivy pressed.

"I know that there are three trials she must pass," her dad answered. "Olivia," he asked, "do you think your parents will allow you to sleep at our house on Friday night?"

"I think so," Olivia said. "Why?"

"That is the appointed date and time for your initiation."

"But that only gives her one night to prepare!" Ivy objected.

Her father studied Olivia's face. "The best and only way to prepare," he said solemnly, "is for you to be ready to bare your true soul."

"What if she doesn't pass?" Ivy asked in a small voice.

He peered down at her, and Ivy couldn't tell whether his eyes were filled with hope or hopelessness. "If it is meant to be," he said in a resigned voice as he turned away to descend the steps, "then it shall be."

CHAPTER 10

On Friday evening, Olivia's mom dropped her off in front of the Vegas' house. Luckily, her mom had a bridge game, so she couldn't even attempt to come inside.

When Olivia rang the bell, Ivy opened the door at once. Inside the foyer, Mr. Vega greeted Olivia with a solemn nod. No one spoke, and then Olivia heard footsteps approaching briskly from down the hall. Into the light of the foyer stepped a tall vampire woman wearing a black and red kimono. It took Olivia a second to realize what was so striking about her. Then she saw what it was. The woman wasn't wearing the contact lenses most vampires used all the time to protect their eyes from the sun and disguise their eye color, and she had *red eyes*.

"I am Valencia Deborg," the woman declared. There was a ruffle of her enormous sleeves, and a thick black binder appeared in one hand, while a ballpoint pen materialized in the other. She clicked the pen meaningfully. "Secretary of human relations for the Vampire Round Table."

"And I," said a nasal voice from the darkness, "am Mr. Boros of ASHH." Olivia half expected a tall, mustachioed vampire to appear in a black cape. Instead, a short bald man in a rumpled suit stepped into the light beside his colleague.

"I saw that guy leaving ASHH right before we snuck in!" Ivy whispered in Olivia's ear.

"And I saw you sneak in on the security cameras," said the man coolly, "right after I left."

Ivy and Olivia both straightened to attention.

"We are here to supervise the initiation of Olivia Abbott," Valencia Deborg said solemnly. "The trials shall commence in one hour, at the setting of the sun."

Casting a sidelong glance toward her sister,

Olivia could see Ivy looked totally worried, which made her feel even more nervous.

"Before we begin"—Mr. Boros held up a stubby white finger—"we must be clear about what is to occur. There are fewer than a dozen humans in the world who know the Blood Secret, all under exceptional circumstances."

"And your circumstances," Ms. Deborg said, training her fiery eyes on Olivia, "are the most exceptional of all."

"Unprecedented, according to our records," confirmed Mr. Boros in his nasal voice.

"The tests to which you are to be subjected were devised hundreds of years ago," Ms. Deborg told Olivia. "They were used only in those rare instances when a human learned the Blood Secret and there was a vampire willing to vouch for him. Is there a vampire present willing to bear this burden?"

"I will," Ivy and her father said at the same time. Olivia could see that her sister was as surprised as she was by Mr. Vega's volunteering like that.

Ms. Deborg and Mr. Boros nodded at each

other, and Ms. Deborg continued. "The original tests were torturous . . ."

"Hideous," said Mr. Boros with a shudder, as Olivia felt the color drain from her face.

"And unspeakably painful," Ms. Deborg concluded.

"But now, of course," Mr. Boros added casually, "the tests are more ritualized."

A sigh of relief escaped from Olivia's mouth. "In the past," Ms. Deborg explained, "if applicants proved unworthy, they were summarily killed. Since the 1926 Vampiric Accord, that is no longer the way."

"So what happens if I fail?" Olivia asked nervously.

"Your memory of anything and everything vampire related will be erased, and you will never see or have any contact with your sister ever again," Mr. Boros answered simply.

"What?" Ivy and Olivia both exclaimed.

"How is that possible?" Olivia asked.

"Vampire scientists have developed a concoction for this purpose," Ms. Deborg answered.

"I understand it's not unlike a strawberry

smoothie," Mr. Boros remarked proudly, "which is much less messy than the old method of removing a portion of the cranial cortex."

"And I wouldn't be able to remember Ivy at all?" Olivia demanded. The vampire officials nodded.

"B-but we just found each other," Ivy stammered.

"Perhaps it is for the best that you and I are moving to Europe," Ivy's father said under his breath.

Ivy shot him a bitter look. "What if Olivia refuses to be initiated?" she asked Ms. Deborg.

"She will confront the same result as one who has failed," Ms. Deborg said icily.

Olivia took a deep breath. "And if I pass the tests?"

"Then everything will continue as before," Mr. Boros replied.

Olivia squeezed her sister's hand. "I know I'm worthy," she whispered bravely. "I'll pass any test they throw at me. I'm not going to lose you."

Of course, inside, Olivia was totally freaking out. Sure, she'd been nervous, but she hadn't had a clue how serious this whole initiation thing was. She was only thirteen, and already she was facing senility.

"Any questions?" Mr. Boros asked.

When Olivia shook her head, Ms. Deborg announced, "The applicant will now have a few moments for solitary contemplation before the First Test begins." She and Mr. Boros turned to leave the room.

"Can I stay with her?" Ivy blurted.

Ms. Deborg stopped abruptly. Without turning around, she said, "I suppose," with a hint of disapproval. Then she and Mr. Boros disappeared down the hallway, while Ivy's father silently bowed his head and climbed the stairs.

In the living room, Ivy wrapped Olivia in a hug. "I'm sorry I got you into this," she said. "I don't know how you could ever forgive me."

Somehow, seeing Ivy so torn up made Olivia feel less dire. "Forgive you?" Olivia said. "You're the coolest thing that ever happened to me."

Ivy responded with a familiar eye roll.

"Are you kidding?" Olivia answered, straightening her pink sweatshirt. "What do you think—I find out I have a vampire twin all the time? Besides," she went on, "if this is really about whether I'm worthy to know the vampire secret, then we don't have anything to worry about. I have a right to know. After all, it's where I came from, too." *Whoa,* Olivia thought. *That all actually makes sense.* All of a sudden, she wasn't so afraid of the tests.

"No matter what," Ivy said in a determined voice, "I won't let them do anything grim to you. Even if something happens, I'll figure out a way to stop them from erasing your memory. I'm not leaving your side for a second."

"Sounds good," Olivia grinned.

Ivy got a mischievous look in her eye, and Olivia could almost hear the gears turning inside her sister's head. "There's a secret escape passageway in the back of the pantry, and we could always sneak you out that way." She started waving her black-nailed hands in the air. "We could even switch if we had to. We could run down to my room right now and put on matching outfits!"

Olivia put her hand gently on her sister's arm. "I'm not going to run, Ivy," she said. "I'm going to do what it takes to pass. I'm going to prove I'm worthy of the Blood Secret once and for all."

"We shall see," a cool voice intoned. Nearly jumping out of her sneakers, Olivia turned to see that Valencia Deborg had appeared in the doorway. "The time has come for the First Test," she announced.

Olivia and Ivy exchanged nervous glances. Ms. Deborg gestured for them to follow her, and before Olivia knew it the vampire official was disappearing down the hall. On the main stairs, Olivia and Ivy had to take the steps two at a time to catch up.

Ms. Deborg led them to the same guest room that had the bathroom where they'd done their final shots for *Vamp* magazine. Against one wall was what looked like a dresser covered by a dark purple velvet sheet. Valencia Deborg pulled the sheet off with a flourish, revealing a black lacquered coffin.

"The Test of Darkness!" she announced dramatically. Olivia's heart flooded with fear. *Who's in there?* she thought. When she glanced at her sister, Ivy just shrugged nervously.

"You must spend the entire night in this coffin," Ms. Deborg explained at last, "from dusk until dawn."

"No way," Olivia said under her breath.

"Way," Ms. Deborg replied without a hint of humor. She glanced toward the window, where the sun had already begun setting. "There is not much time," she said, and gestured for Olivia to go change.

A minute later, Olivia was standing alone in front of the same ornate mirror where she'd stood posing with her sister, except this time she was alone, wearing her sunflower pajamas, and brushing her teeth nervously.

I don't want to be shut in a box all night, she thought, *even if it does have a plush velvet interior . . . but I don't want to lose my sister even more.*

When she emerged from the bathroom, Ivy and Ms. Deborg were waiting beside the open coffin expectantly. A laugh escaped from Ivy's mouth.

"What?" Olivia inquired.

"Killer pajamas," Ivy teased.

"It is time," Ms. Deborg interrupted.

Olivia walked up to the coffin. There was a little step stool to help her up, and she climbed inside. She lay down on her back and tucked her clammy hands at her sides.

"Does this thing have a nightlight?" she tried to joke.

Instead of answering, Ms. Deborg pulled down the lid. The last thing Olivia saw was her sister's worried face, and then . . . nothing but darkness.

Olivia strained to hear her sister's or Ms. Deborg's voice outside the coffin, but it was eerily silent. All she could hear was her own panicked breathing. She tried to make out the ruffles in the upholstery that she knew were inches from her face, but she couldn't. She raised a shaking hand slowly to touch the lid.

You're okay, she told herself. *It's just the dark. Nothing can hurt you.* Her mind started to wander. *You're just in a coffin. Used by vampires. Who happen to drink blood.* Suddenly she could hear the loud, quick thuds of her own heart beating, and she had the urge to throw open the coffin and run out of the house screaming.

Instead, Olivia decided to try not to focus on

where she was and count sheep. At first, they were all white. Then, without even thinking about it, they became black sheep. And, pretty soon, they started flying.

By the time she got to thirty-four, Olivia realized she was counting bats—which, for some reason, gave her the worst case of the giggles ever.

In an effort to stop her mind from playing tricks on her, Olivia tried to think of nice people: Ivy, her parents, Camilla, Sophia. After a few seconds, she felt herself relaxing. Actually, the coffin was surprisingly comfortable. She even had enough room to turn on her side. She started worrying about what tomorrow's tests were going to be, but then she thought, *I thought this test was going to be a total nightmare, but it's not so bad,* and felt herself drifting off to sleep.

CHAPTER 11

Olivia was awakened suddenly by a flood of light. She covered her eyes with her hands, peeking out between her fingers.

Out of the corner of her eyes she registered that she was surrounded by purple velvet and absentmindedly started rubbing her toe against it. Then she saw a black-lacquered edge, which made her think of Mr. Vega's decorating. She lazily turned her head from side to side. *I slept pretty well,* she thought with a yawn, *considering I'm in a coffin.*

The pale, gaunt face of Valencia Deborg appeared above her. The vampire's lips were moving, but for a second Olivia couldn't work out what she was saying. "Olivia Abbott," she finally made out, "you have passed the First Test, the Test of Darkness."

Olivia sat upright and clapped like she'd just finished a cheer. She looked around to catch her sister's eye, but Ms. Deborg was the only person there.

"Once you have changed, report to the upstairs landing," Ms. Deborg said sternly before sweeping out of the room.

Olivia rushed to wash her face, brush her teeth, and throw on her clothes. She raced down the hall to the stairs, expecting to see Ivy. Instead, Mr. Boros was standing there alone.

"Good morning," he said. The few remaining hairs on his head were sticking out at all angles and he was wearing the same rumpled suit he'd worn yesterday. Olivia figured he must have slept in an extra coffin in the attic or something.

Olivia followed him down the stairs to the breakfast room, where Valencia Deborg was ready, wearing a fresh dark-red and purple kimono and holding a tall glass filled with pink frothy liquid. "Your breakfast."

Olivia's heart jumped. *It's the memory-erasure concoction!* "But I thought I passed!" she sputtered.

Ms. Deborg frowned. "You would rather have Marshmallow Platelets?"

"No," Olivia said, "but I don't want to drink a memory-loss smoothie, either."

Ms. Deborg and Mr. Boros both looked at her cluelessly.

"Oh!" Mr. Boros said finally. "She thinks . . . No, no, young lady, this is a *real* strawberry smoothie. Made especially for you."

"Really?" Olivia peered into the glass.

"Cross my neck and hope to die," Ms. Deborg pledged without smiling.

Sitting down, Olivia took a tentative sip. It was superdelicious. All at once she realized she was ravenous and began gulping through the straw.

Halfway through, she started to get a brain freeze headache that made her take a break. "Where's Ivy?" she wondered aloud.

Mr. Boros and Ms. Deborg exchanged glances. "She's not here," Mr. Boros said.

"Where'd she go?" Olivia asked.

"How should we know?" Ms. Deborg answered blankly.

Olivia ducked her head to finish her smoothie. *That's strange,* she thought. *Ivy promised she'd stay close by. Maybe she's working on one of those contingency plans of hers, like preparing an escape route out a second-floor window.*

After her smoothie, Ms. Deborg presented Olivia with a piece of toast with red jam. As Olivia ate it, she started to get nervous for her next test. *Don't worry,* she told herself. *Ivy will definitely be back for that.* She ate her toast more and more slowly until just a few bites were left. She didn't want to finish it until her sister showed up. Finally, Ms. Deborg took the plate away and gestured for Olivia to follow her and Mr. Boros. They led her back up to the second floor and down the hall to Mr. Vega's study.

As the vampire officials proceeded into the room ahead of her, Olivia could see Mr. Vega waiting in the corner next to the enormous globe. She froze in the doorway and scanned the rest of the room. Ivy wasn't there. She planted her feet.

"I want to know where Ivy is," she demanded.

Ms. Deborg glared down at her. "I told you; we don't know where she is."

"I don't believe you," Olivia said. Everybody just stared at her.

Ivy's father cleared his throat. "Ivy mentioned that she was going out with Brendan for the morning. She said she'd be back in time for the Third Test." He looked away.

Ms. Deborg ruffled an enormous kimono sleeve and a sleek black watch appeared on her slender wrist. She looked at it impatiently. "We must proceed with the Second Test at once."

Olivia shook her head. "Ivy promised she'd stay with me. She wouldn't break a promise like that."

"Are you saying you are unwilling to proceed?" Mr. Boros asked sternly.

Olivia hesitated. *Ivy swore she'd be here,* she thought, *and she's not. What if they've done something to her?*

"I guess I am." Olivia gulped. "At least, I am until Ivy shows up."

There was silence. Then Olivia thought she

saw the slightest hint of a smile appear on Mr. Vega's face.

"Olivia Abbott," Ms. Deborg announced, "you have passed the Second Test, the Test of Faith."

"Huh?" Olivia said. Mr. Boros slipped out of the room and returned with Ivy, who looked more frustrated than a cheerleader who had fallen during a tumbling routine.

"They wouldn't let me in!" Ivy shook Mr. Boros off and ran up to Olivia. "Are you okay?"

"I'm okay," Olivia said. "Are you okay?"

"Uh-huh," Ivy answered.

"I was so worried!" Olivia told her.

Ivy nodded in agreement. "What happened?"

"I passed the Second Test." Olivia shrugged.

"The Test of Faith," Mr. Boros said in his nasal voice, "is passed when the applicant shows complete faith in the vampire who vouched for her."

"I knew something was wrong," Olivia began, "because you said—"

"I wouldn't leave your side for a second." Ivy grinned. She and Olivia high-fived. "Only one more nail to seal this coffin!" Ivy said excitedly.

"The Third, and final, Test," Ms. Deborg said

solemnly, "is the Test of Blood."

Olivia clutched her stomach. The thought of drinking blood totally made her want to puke. "You mean I have to drink . . . ?" She couldn't even bring herself to finish the question.

"That would be a Test of Fortitude, wouldn't it?" Ms. Deborg deadpanned.

"Of course we'd never make a human drink blood," assured Mr. Boros. "No, no, the Test of Blood merely refers to *your* blood, Olivia."

"What?" Olivia croaked.

Valencia ruffled a sleeve, revealing a huge ruby ring that glinted on her finger. She approached Olivia and pressed the sides of the enormous ring. The ruby popped open to reveal what looked like the sharp point of a thumbtack. Ms. Deborg extended her other hand, palm up, expectantly.

Olivia took a step backward. "What do I have to do?"

Instead of answering, Ms. Deborg curled the tips of her fingers invitingly.

Olivia reached behind her back and gripped Ivy's hand for moral support. Then she shut her eyes tight and reached out with her free hand. She felt Valencia Deborg's cool fingers close around her index finger.

"What's happening?" she whispered, terrified.

"Don't hurt her!" Ivy cried.

But then nothing happened. Mr. Boros cleared his throat meaningfully a few times, and eventually Olivia realized that he was trying to get her attention. She forced herself to open her eyes and saw that he was holding up a yellowed piece of parchment inches from her face. Its borders were filled with elaborate, spiky designs, and in the center was a poem written in fancy black script.

"The applicant will read the Blood Oath," he declared.

Olivia took a deep breath before starting to read aloud.

> "*Their Night is my Night.*
> *Their Blood is my Blood.*
> *Their Secret is my Secret.*
> *This Oath is my Coffin.*'"

Underneath the words, where a line for her signature might be, was a small blank circle.

Valencia Deborg looked at her meaningfully, still grasping Olivia's index finger in one hand as she held up her needle-tipped ring in the other.

Olivia saw that Ivy was smiling proudly. Sort of surprisingly, so was Ivy's father. Olivia nodded bravely at Ms. Deborg as Mr. Boros positioned the paper underneath her hand.

The vampire touched her ring to the tip of Olivia's finger. Olivia winced, and a drop of blood bloomed like a tiny rose. She let it drip off her finger, and it landed with a tiny splatter in the middle of the parchment circle.

"Olivia Abbott has passed all three tests in her initiation," Ms. Deborg pronounced. "The Blood Secret is hers to keep."

Olivia and Ivy shared the biggest hug ever, and everybody started clapping—even Ivy's father and Valencia Deborg. Then the vampire officials led them all downstairs to the living room, where Olivia was shocked to find Sophia, Brendan, Bethany, and Mr. and Mrs. Daniels. They all erupted into applause the moment Olivia walked into the room.

"Bravo!" Brendan shouted. "A-positive, Olivia!"

Bethany hooted like a crazed owl.

Olivia just stood there, beaming.

"Everyone who knows you know the secret is in this room," Ivy whispered in her ear.

Sophia started snapping pictures like crazy. Ivy tried to step away, but Sophia begged her to stay there and try to act natural. "I'm hoping *Vamp* magazine will want these pictures for their 'Stalking the Undead' celebrity candid column!" she said excitedly.

Valencia Deborg stepped into the center of the room and held up her slender hands. "As you've guessed, Olivia Abbott has successfully completed the sacred rites of initiation. She is officially sanctioned into our community by the Vampire Round Table."

"And by ASHH as well," Mr. Boros piped up from near the door.

Everybody started clapping again, and then they all sang this bizarre song in some weird language that sounded like "For She's a Jolly Good Fellow" played backward. Olivia swayed to the music, feeling simultaneously awed and bemused by the whole display.

Ivy was so happy and relieved that her sister had passed the tests, she almost felt like wearing pink! Everyone was milling around Olivia, congratulating her and joking around. Meanwhile, Ivy's father appeared, holding a silver tray loaded with crystal flutes of deep red A neg. He handed them out, until the only one left had a pink-and-white polka-dotted cocktail umbrella sticking out of it.

"For Olivia," he said, holding out the tray, "some cranberry juice. The little umbrella was to keep the glasses from getting mixed up."

Ivy's heart cracked open like a coffin at dawn. *Maybe he's finally starting to accept Olivia now that she's an honorary vamp,* she thought.

A few minutes later, Ivy spied her father sitting alone in the corner, sipping his cocktail. She crept over to Olivia and gently tugged her away from Mr. and Mrs. Daniels.

"You should go talk to my dad," Ivy said. "I think he's finally started to see you for who you really are."

Her sister approached him tentatively. "Thanks

so much for the party, Mr. Vega," Ivy heard her say.

Her father looked up, startled, as if Olivia had woken him from a dream. He stood up abruptly, nearly knocking Olivia's glass from her hand, and a bit of cranberry juice sloshed over the edge of the glass and onto the floor.

"I'm so sorry," he blurted. "I have to . . ." He shot a desperate look in Ivy's direction but immediately looked away. "Please excuse me." And with that, he rushed from the room.

Olivia shrugged at Ivy disappointedly before kneeling to wipe up the cranberry juice with her napkin.

Ivy sighed. Her father still couldn't deal with Olivia, and he was probably still mad at Ivy for breaking into ASHH. But that was all dirt and worms compared to the way he'd been acting. *Why can't he understand that I deserve to find out about my real parents?* she thought. *Why can't he make more of an effort with my blood sister?*

Ivy walked into the kitchen, half looking for her father. Her dad wasn't in there, but she did notice that he'd put a tray of tiny pastries filled with ground meat in the oven. She was opening the oven to check on them when Brendan's parents came into the kitchen with Bethany.

"I'm gonna be the most popular girl at Franklin Grove Elementary once everyone finds out that I go to parties with Ivy and Olivia, the two coolest girls ever!" Bethany chattered. "They'll probably want to do a piece on me in *Vamp*!" She sucked in her cheeks like she was posing for a fashion shoot. Meanwhile, Mrs. Daniels reached into her purse and pulled out a little white bottle.

"Time for your VitaVamp, sweetheart," she said.

"Ew!" Bethany said.

"You can have it in your A neg," her mother told her, splitting the capsule in two and letting the black powder drop into the glass, where it fizzed lightly before dissolving.

"It tastes worse than broccoli!" Bethany protested.

"Don't you want to grow up to be a strong vampire?" Ivy tried.

"No," Bethany answered. "I want to grow up to be a cheerleader like Olivia."

They all laughed.

Mr. Daniels stroked his chin. "Ivy, do you think I might have one of those cocktail umbrellas?"

"Sure," said Ivy, picking one out of the box on the counter and handing it over.

"That's just like Olivia's!" Bethany squealed. "Can I have one? Please can I have one?"

"You may if you're willing to drink up your A neg," said Mr. Daniels.

"Okay!" Bethany agreed.

Brendan's dad dropped the umbrella in the glass, and his mom handed it over to Bethany, who sipped at it demurely. "Totally yummy!" she declared and skipped out of the kitchen.

★ 🐰 ★

Olivia was sitting on the black leather living room couch with Brendan, talking about their social studies teacher Ms. Starling's strange obsession with the guillotine, when Bethany bounded over.

"Olivia, darling," she said like a high society diva, "you look absolutely marvelous." Olivia giggled.

"Bethany," called Mrs. Daniels with a smile, "why don't you tell Olivia about the latest fashion at your school?"

"Let me guess," Olivia said. "Dressing up like opposite twins?"

"No way," Bethany sang. "That's *soooo* last week." She gingerly put down her glass on the coffee table next to Olivia's. "The latest is to dress half Goth"—Bethany held out one hand, on which all of her fingernails were painted black—"and half bunny!" She held out her other hand to reveal that the nails were all pink.

Olivia nodded, impressed. Then she had an idea. "You could even try alternating nails—black, pink, black, pink, black."

"Oh, my gosh!" Bethany gasped. "You are a total genius! I'm going to do that, like, the moment I get home!"

"Oh, really?" Mrs. Daniels said skeptically.

"Please, Mom, can I?" Bethany pleaded.

Olivia suddenly realized she hadn't seen her sister in a while. "Have either of you seen Ivy?" she asked.

"In the kitchen," Mrs. Daniels answered.

176

Olivia seized the opportunity to grab her flute of cranberry juice off the table and head off to check on her sister. As she walked, she sipped at her drink. In all honesty, it wasn't very good cranberry juice—it tasted sort of like overcooked broccoli—but she was parched. She took a big gulp so she wouldn't have to taste it.

Ivy was just finishing laying finger foods on a square black tray.

"Hey." Olivia smiled, but as she said it the whole room seemed to go crooked. She put a hand on the counter to steady herself.

"Are you all right?" Ivy asked.

"I don't know," Olivia replied, "but there seems to be two of you." *And my legs feel like Jell-O,* she thought.

Both of the Ivys she could see rushed over and helped Olivia into a chair. Olivia blinked hard.

"Still seeing double?" Ivy asked.

"No," Olivia croaked. "Now there's three of you."

Suddenly, three Bethanys appeared in the doorway. Each one was holding Olivia's drink with its polka-dotted umbrella.

"That's my drink," Olivia said, realizing that she was thirstier than ever.

"Olivia," Ivy said slowly, "you're already holding your drink."

"Uh-oh," said all the Bethanys.

"Bethany," requested Ivy in an urgent voice, "can you go get Sophia?"

"But—"

"Now!" Ivy said.

"Not so loud." Olivia winced. All these voices were hurting her head.

"Olivia," Ivy said, and there were four of her now. "Listen to me. Your drink got switched with Bethany's."

"You mean I drank blood?" Olivia heard herself say dumbly.

"Among other things," Ivy told her.

Suddenly the voice that was supposed to be her own started talking and Olivia couldn't stop it. "Am I growing fangs? Am I a bat? Do I get my own coffin?" Each question echoed the moment it was spoken, and soon it seemed like a bunch of people who sounded just like her were talking over one another inside her head.

Then, for some reason, all those Olivias started laughing hysterically.

★ 🦇 ★

As far as Ivy knew, drinking A neg shouldn't really have any effect on a human other than grossing them out. So it must have been Bethany's VitaVamp that was making her sister act like it was a full moon.

Ivy noticed that Mrs. Daniels had left the vitamin bottle on the counter, and she snatched it up to scan the label. "'Warning,'" she read. "'Not for human use. If ingested by a human, dizziness, nausea, and hallucinations may result for up to eight hours.'"

Ivy went and knelt beside her sister, whose laughter had given way to a dreamy song about bunny rabbits. "Good news, Olivia," Ivy said. "Worst-case scenario: you'll hallucinate for the rest of the day."

Olivia stopped singing and nodded. "Your kitchen is sparkly," she said happily. Then she sprang to her feet and started spinning with her head flung back.

"Are you okay?" Ivy asked nervously.

179

"I'm great!" Olivia squealed. She clawed at the air until she found Ivy's arm. "Let's go back to the party!"

With a jolt, Ivy realized that that was the worst idea since the wooden stake. *Olivia can't go back in there,* she thought. *What if the secretary of human affairs for the Vampire Round Table and the top ASHH agent see her like this and have second thoughts?* She had to get Olivia to the basement until she was acting like a human again.

Ivy looked toward the doorway desperately. She needed Sophia's help if she was going to successfully transport her sister downstairs.

"Olivia?" Ivy said.

Olivia looked all around. "I hear someone calling my name!" she whispered in wonderment.

"Olivia," Ivy repeated, sitting her back down in her chair, "I need you to stay right here for a second. Okay?"

"Okeydoke," chirped Olivia, planting her hands in her lap like a kindergartner.

Ivy darted back toward the living room. Just outside the door, she bumped smack into Sophia.

"What did you say to Bethany?" Sophia asked.

"She said you yelled at her."

Ivy shook her head. "It's Olivia," she whispered. "She drank Bethany's drink by accident. It had VitaVamp in it!"

Sophia's eyes widened. "Did she barf?"

"Worse," Ivy said. "She's temporarily lost her mind! You have to help me get her to my room!" She dragged Sophia after her to the kitchen.

Olivia's chair was sitting there empty, and all at once Ivy's chest felt like somebody had shoveled it full of coal. "Olivia?" she called. No answer. She said a little prayer and looked in the broom closet, but the only thing in there was the broom.

"Where is she?" said Sophia.

"I lost her," Ivy gulped. She ran to the front hall, uncertain where she should look next. Sophia followed closely.

"Shhh!" Sophia said suddenly. "I hear something."

Ivy froze, listening intently. From upstairs, she heard the faint sounds of her sister singing loopily. She bounded up the front stairs with Sophia right behind her. Olivia was prancing around the second floor hallway, her hands over her head.

"Olivia!" Ivy called in a whisper.

"I'm a bunny!" Olivia whispered and then turned and wiggled her backside. "Hop! Hop! Hop!" she said, and bounced away.

"Olivia!" Ivy called again, chasing her.

Ivy and Sophia had almost caught up to her when Olivia suddenly stopped in front of the open door of Ivy's father's study, mesmerized by something inside. Ivy lunged for her, but Olivia hopped away at the last moment, and Ivy ended up belly flopping onto the floor.

Ouch! Ivy winced. Raising herself to her knees, she glanced inside the study.

Her father was standing rigidly behind his desk, his hands flat on its surface. He almost looked pink. Ivy quickly got to her feet.

"Ivy," her father said, his voice shaking, "this floor is no place for your guests to horse around!"

"Olivia isn't a guest," Ivy snapped. "She's my sister." She felt like screaming, *Why is it so hard for you to accept her?* but she knew she'd better take Olivia away before her father realized what kind of shape she was in. She marched down the hall to Olivia and gently took her arm. "Come on."

"But my ring's there," Olivia mumbled, nodding toward the study.

Ivy glanced down at her sister's hand and was relieved to see that her emerald ring was still securely on her finger. "It's right here," she said quietly. Sophia got on the other side of Olivia, and together they started guiding her slowly back down the hallway. Ivy didn't even look at her father as they passed his study again.

They were finally making their way down the main staircase when Ivy saw Mr. Daniels charging up the steps toward them. For a split second, Ivy considered trying to make a three-legged run for it. Instead she just shot a resigned look over Olivia's shoulder at Sophia.

"Bethany told me what happened," Mr. Daniels said, reaching up to Olivia's face and pulling open one of her eyelids with his thumb.

"You have hair like Einstein." Olivia giggled.

"Let's get her to the kitchen," Mr. Daniels said professionally. "Ivy, if you'll help me find the ingredients, we should be able to create an antidote."

Now why can't my dad be more like Brendan's? Ivy thought gratefully.

In Ivy's front foyer, Olivia was saying good-bye to the last of the guests. Except for the half hour or so when apparently she'd been completely embarrassing, it had been a super party. Valencia Deborg solemnly produced a tiny V-shaped pin from one of her sleeves and pinned it to Olivia's sweatshirt before sweeping out the door. Mr. Boros pumped her hand proudly. As for the Danielses, she felt like she'd known them forever. Mrs. Daniels hoped she'd agree to babysit for Bethany and promised to be in charge of the veggie burgers in future.

Still, something kept niggling at the back of Olivia's mind. It felt like there was something she'd been meaning to say since the moment she'd returned to her senses, but she just couldn't remember what it was.

Sophia came up and gave her a hug. "Remind me to bring VitaVamp to your next party," she teased. "You can be the entertainment."

"Thanks," Olivia said sheepishly.

Soon it was just Olivia and Ivy, plus Ivy's dad, who was looming back by the staircase. Olivia glanced at her watch; her parents were expecting her home in twenty minutes.

"I guess I'd better get going, too," she said to her sister.

Ivy nodded. Olivia turned toward the stairs. "Thank you for everything, Mr. Vega."

"You're welcome, Olivia," he said expressionlessly. For a split second, Olivia caught his dark eyes, and in a flash, she remembered what it was that she had seen when she was under the influence of Bethany's pill.

He turned to ascend the stairs, and the moment he was out of sight, Olivia pulled her sister close.

"Your father was looking at a wooden box in his study."

Ivy shrugged. "My dad has lots of wooden boxes."

"But this one had our symbol on it," Olivia said, raising her hand to show Ivy her ring.

"Olivia," Ivy said, rolling her eyes, "you were imagining things. You were out of it."

"I saw it, Ivy," Olivia said firmly. "I know I did. I walked past the study, and he was sitting at his desk with this box open in front of him. He was reading something. And I saw—I remember it totally—our symbol was carved on the box's lid!"

Ivy bit her lip. "But why would my dad have something with our symbol on it?"

Olivia shook her head after a moment. "I don't know," she admitted.

Ivy sighed. "He did seem freaked out when he realized we were up there," she recalled.

"Something strange is going on," Olivia decided, and she could tell that her sister didn't need any convincing. "We need to find that box, Ivy."

"Well, there's nothing we can do with my dad around," Ivy said thoughtfully. "But he's going out tomorrow morning. Can you come back first thing?"

Olivia nodded. She hugged her sister tight before setting off for home. Ivy's long driveway descended toward the street like a giant question mark—and Olivia couldn't help feeling that tomorrow, when she walked back up it the other way, she'd arrive at some answers at last.

CHAPTER 12

Olivia crept up to her sister's house early Sunday morning, the shadows of willow branches reaching out at her eerily. Even though Mr. Vega's car was already gone from its spot beside the house, she hesitated beside the porch. Somehow it didn't seem right to just walk up in broad daylight and ring the doorbell when she and Ivy were about to snoop around inside. She decided to go around back.

Kneeling beside her sister's bedroom window, she saw Ivy pacing the floor of her room below. Olivia rapped on the glass with her knuckles, and Ivy jumped, clearly startled. Then she rushed up the stairs and opened the window.

Olivia clambered through onto the basement stair landing.

"You scared me to death!" said Ivy.

"I thought vampires were already dead," Olivia joked.

"Ha-ha. Very funny," Ivy replied.

Two seconds later, Olivia was following Ivy up to Mr. Vega's study. Her sister immediately began rummaging through the enormous mahogany desk, Olivia started with a shelf in the corner filled with tiny drawers. She felt a little awkward about snooping through Mr. Vega's things, but she was certain she'd seen the Lazar symbol yesterday and she needed to know why Mr. Vega had something with that symbol on it.

The first drawer was packed with gray fabric swatches. The second had nothing but little metal plates—none of them with the Lazar symbol on them. The third drawer was filled with mini-gargoyles.

A half hour later, the sisters still hadn't found the wooden box, and Olivia was starting to get discouraged. There were countless urns, vases, busts, drawers, boxes, and pedestals. The box could be *anywhere*.

Ivy began circling the room like a caged panther. Suddenly she stopped and slapped her palm against her forehead. "I'm such a fruit bat!" she exclaimed. Then she walked to the front of the desk, where a bunch of files were propped up between two brass gargoyle bookends. She twisted the head of the bookend on the right, and across the room two bookshelves sank back into the wall and slid apart to reveal a dim passageway.

"Cool!" Olivia said, following Ivy eagerly into the shadows. She found herself descending a tightly wound spiral staircase. "Where are we?" she whispered.

"Between the kitchen and the living room," Ivy explained. "This passageway is the only entrance to this room."

The steps ended at the floor of a tiny circular room. Row after row of small, shallow gravestone-shaped holes were carved into the walls. Instead of holding bones, each one held books and scrolls.

"My father's special collection," Ivy announced.

189

Olivia crept up and peered into one of the hollows. It was sealed with a pane of glass, and inside she saw a marble tablet carved with mysterious hieroglyphics. Alongside it was stretched an ancient-looking scroll that looked like a blueprint.

"What is all this?" she whispered.

"My dad's old decorating textbooks," answered Ivy from over her shoulder.

Ivy started combing through some books in a hollow across the room, while Olivia gravitated to a nearby stone recess. She pulled down a fat black book with a cracked spine and discovered it was a photograph album.

Olivia's mouth fell open with shock. There was a picture of her as a little girl, wearing a witch's hat and holding a broom! *I don't remember ever wearing that for Halloween,* she thought. Then she realized that of course she was looking at pictures of Ivy, and she started to giggle.

"Remember when I said next time we'll look at pictures of *you* drooling and wearing embarrassing clothes?" Olivia reminded Ivy, starting to flip through the album excitedly. "Well, the time has come!"

Ivy winced. "Aren't you supposed to be looking for our box?"

Olivia was about to slide the album back into place, when something caught her eye at the back of the recess. It looked like there was something else there. Something brown. She pulled out another album and reached in curiously.

Olivia's pulse quickened as she felt a wooden edge. Slowly, carefully, she pulled out the box hidden there on its side. Without Olivia having said anything, Ivy appeared beside her. They both looked down at the gilded symbol on the lid—the same symbol that was on their rings.

It's the box I saw yesterday, Olivia thought, her heart pounding. She heard Ivy's breath catch.

Olivia lifted the lid and they stared down at a stack of yellowed papers inside. Ivy lifted out the top sheet by its edges, as if she was scared it would crumble to dust, and turned it over.

"'My love,'" Ivy began reading, but then she stopped. Olivia followed her sister's gaze to the bottom of the page. The letter was signed, *Forever yours, Susannah.*

"Why would my dad have a letter from our

biological mother?" Ivy wondered aloud. Olivia thumbed quickly through the papers and saw that they all seemed to be letters from Susannah. Underneath the stack was a smaller piece of shiny paper with scalloped edges. On it, in neat script, were the words, *Susannah and I on our wedding day.*

Slowly, carefully, Olivia picked up the small piece of paper and flipped it over. She could barely believe what she was looking at. It was a picture of her parents.

Susannah wore a long, white lace bridal gown with an elegant scooped neckline, and her face was alight with a mischievous smile that reminded Olivia of Ivy. The picture must have been taken a long time ago, because all the colors in the picture were sort of brownish. Beside her, clutching her hand, stood the tall, broad-shouldered groom in a black tuxedo with a skinny black bow tie. He had a huge black mustache and longish hair and was grinning toothily at the camera.

"It's our father," Olivia whispered.

"Let me see!" said Ivy, taking the picture and

holding it up in the dim light. Ivy blinked, and Olivia saw something change on her sister's face.

"It's my dad," Ivy whispered.

Olivia nodded automatically: *Yes, our biological dad,* she thought. Then, all at once, she understood what her sister had really meant. She snatched the picture back.

Behind the unkempt hair and the weird mustache, the grinning groom in the photograph was none other than Charles Vega.

★ 🦇 ★

Ivy felt as if her head were a cave suddenly crowded with bats. "My dad didn't *adopt* me," she heard herself say. "He's my *real dad*."

"And *my* real dad," Olivia echoed in a faraway voice.

The two of them stood there, stunned and silent for a long moment.

That's why there was no record of my adoption at the agency, Ivy realized. All her life, she'd wondered what her biological father was like, and now she saw that she'd known the answer all along. She felt her heart swell, and a wave of happiness crashed over her. "*My* dad is *our* dad," she said.

There were tears in Olivia's eyes. They began trading the wedding picture back and forth.

"I can't believe he ever had a mustache like that," Ivy marveled.

"He was in hiding," Olivia said with mock offense. "Hey, look," she went on, pointing to the happy couple's clasped hands. "They're wearing rings just like ours!"

Ivy's mouth fell open. "Those aren't *like* ours," she realized. "Those *are* ours. We're wearing our parents' wedding rings!" She touched the ring on the chain around her neck, and for the first time she understood why her ring was too big, while Olivia's fit perfectly: Ivy had their father's wedding band, Olivia had their mother's.

"Of course." Olivia sighed like they always should have known.

It must be so hard for my dad to see me wearing it every day, Ivy thought tenderly. She remembered how, after her father had given her the ring for her tenth birthday, he'd become very quiet and distracted for a few days.

"So why didn't he just admit he's my dad?" Olivia wondered, looking bewildered. "And why did he always tell you you were adopted?"

"My dad always says he doesn't like looking back at the past," Ivy said. She looked again at the picture of their parents and how happy they seemed together. "Maybe it's just too difficult for him. We remind him of our mom." She smiled at Olivia. "Especially you. You're human like she was."

Olivia couldn't stop looking at their parents' wedding picture. *My dad's been right here all along*, she thought. She felt like a missing piece had been added to her heart, one that she hadn't even known was missing. She remembered the first time she'd met Mr. Vega, when she had been disguised as Ivy and they had been decorating the upstairs ballroom for the All Hallows' Ball together—how sophisticated and stylish and cool he'd seemed. And then she thought of the way he'd offered to vouch for her for her initiation, and how proud he'd looked when she'd passed the tests, and she felt warm inside.

"He'll be home soon," Ivy interrupted her thoughts gently. "We'd better get back upstairs."

Together, the two of them packed the picture and the letters back into the wooden box and returned it to its hiding place. This time, Olivia led the way up the darkened spiral staircase. She wasn't spooked or disoriented at all. Somehow, now, she felt like she was at home.

"Ivy," Olivia began hesitantly as they emerged into the study once more. "Do you mind if we don't tell your dad—I mean, *our* dad—about our discovery just yet?"

Ivy shook her head. "No, it's fine," she replied, squeezing her sister's hand. "I need some time to get my head around this myself."

A few minutes later, Olivia was lying thoughtfully on the floor of the living room when Ivy let out a long, sad sigh from her place on the couch.

"What is it?" Olivia asked, staring at the light gray ceiling.

"I just remembered we're supposed to move to Europe in, like, just over a week," replied Ivy.

Olivia had forgotten, too, and for a moment, she felt like she'd been punched in the gut. *It's bad enough that Ivy's leaving,* she thought. *But now I know I'll be losing my biological father, too!*

She took a deep breath and sat upright. "That means," she said calmly, "we have that long to change our dad's mind!"

Slowly, Ivy's face hardened into a look of determination. "You're right. We have to find a way to talk him out of it."

Just then, Olivia heard the sound of a car pulling up outside. The sisters stood up and smiled at each other.

"Our dad's here," Olivia said thoughtfully. The words "our dad" still felt strange to her.

Ivy nodded, and together they headed to the front door to greet him.

Ivy Vega and her best friend, Sophia Hewitt, hustled through the oldest cemetery in Franklin Grove on their way to school Monday morning. The grassy path, stiff with frost, crunched loudly beneath their heavy boots, and Ivy pushed her hands into the pockets of her full-length, black down jacket to keep them warm.

I'm going to miss this old graveyard when I move to Europe, Ivy thought. Even though it was still a little dark, in the distance she could make out the low silhouette of her boyfriend's family crypt, where she and her friends had spent so much time hanging out. Outside the cemetery gates, the lights of nearby houses twinkled.

"Such a killer party!" Sophia exclaimed, interrupting Ivy's thoughts. It seemed like forever ago, but on Saturday, Ivy's human twin, Olivia, had been initiated into the vampire community, and they'd had a little celebration. "You must be seriously excited," Sophia went on, "that Olivia knowing about vampires isn't a secret anymore. It's all over the Vorld Vide Veb."

Ivy pressed her mouth down into her black knitted scarf and exhaled, warming her neck. *That's not the only thing that isn't a secret any longer*, she thought. "Sophia," she said aloud, "there's something I have to tell you."

Olivia Abbott was met by a hot blast of indoor air as she opened the huge oak front doors of Franklin Grove Middle School. Scanning the lobby, she pulled off her hat and swung it around by one of the pink pom-poms that hung from its earflaps. She jumped up and down to get the cold out. Olivia had worn her cheerleading uniform for a school spirit assembly, but even with leggings, she felt like a popsicle.

Where are you, Camilla? Olivia thought as she hopped from foot to foot, keeping her eyes peeled for her friend. *I have huge news!*

The door to the outside swung open, and Olivia looked over eagerly. Unfortunately, it was just Charlotte Brown, Olivia's snotty cheerleading captain. She was wearing fluffy white earmuffs.

"Hi, Charlotte," Olivia said, unable to keep the disappointment out of her voice. Charlotte let the door swing shut behind her, but her cheerleading cronies, Katie and Alison, hurried in on her heels. They were wearing earmuffs, too.

"Oh, Olivia, I'm so totally cold!" Charlotte whined.

"We're cold, too!" said Katie and Alison, who had a talent for always thinking the same thing as Charlotte.

"Then you'd all better get inside right away and warm up!" Olivia said, switching on her smile. They skipped past without another word.

One person trickled into school after another, and every time the door to the outside opened, Olivia's heart leapt. Finally, she caught sight of Camilla's bouncy blond curls.

"Camilla!" Olivia called.

"Hey," Camilla said, her face breaking into an easy smile when she saw Olivia. "Sorry I'm a little late. You sounded so excited on the phone last night. What's up?"

Olivia grinned. "Only the biggest news of my entire life!"

Camilla looked at her skeptically. "Bigger than finding out you have a long-lost twin sister?"

Olivia wrinkled her nose; Camilla had a point. Olivia and Ivy hadn't even known they each had a twin until Olivia's first day of school in Franklin Grove a few months ago. Come to think of it, the whole "my-sister-is-a-vampire" thing was big news, too, but of course Camilla didn't know anything about that. Olivia was one of the only humans in the world who did.

"Just as big," Olivia decided, pulling Camilla behind the enormous potted ferns in the corner of the lobby

Olivia took a deep breath. "You can't tell anyone," she said. "Promise?"

"Promise," Camilla said solemnly. "Just tell me already!"

★ 🦇 ★

"I *am* telling you," Ivy protested.

"No," Sophia said, "what you're doing is *trying* to tell me. So far you're just sighing a lot."

Ivy sighed again, sending a tiny cloud into the cold air. "I still can't believe it," Ivy murmured by way of explanation.

4

"Ivy," Sophia said sternly, "I'm freezing my fangs off here."

"You don't have fangs," replied Ivy, peering around the cemetery to make sure no one else was lurking nearby. "You file them like the rest of us."

"It's an expression," Sophia said, her voice rising with frustration. "Now tell me your big revelation!"

"I found . . ." Ivy gulped. "Olivia and I found out . . ."

Sophia stared at her impatiently.

"Who my real father is," Ivy blurted at last.

In their fourth fangtastic adventure, Olivia and Ivy must unravel a truly vampalicious mystery!

Twins Ivy and Olivia were stunned to find out that Ivy's dad, Charles Vega, is actually their biological father! Why did he separate them when they were only a year old? The twins are determined to find out their dad's secret, but they have to act fast—Mr. Vega is moving to Europe and he's taking Ivy with him! How can the twins convince him to stay in Franklin Grove?

Don't miss any of the My Sister the Vampire books by Sienna Mercer:

HarperTrophy®
An Imprint of HarperCollinsPublishers

www.harpercollinschildrens.com